Note to Readers

While the Lankford and Allerton families are fictional, the turmoil in Boston leading up to the Revolutionary War is not. By the time war broke out, one in every four people in Boston was a British soldier. These soldiers were everywhere—in people's homes, businesses, and public meetinghouses. Whether citizens were Loyalists or Patriots, most of them wished there were far fewer soldiers in their town.

In spite of all the soldiers, Patriots continued to work secretly for American rights. Will and Stephen are involved in spying and sending coded messages that are typical of the work the Patriots did in this dangerous situation.

✰ The ✰
AMERICAN
REVOLUTION

JoAnn A. Grote

BARBOUR
PUBLISHING, INC.
Uhrichsville, Ohio

To my nephew Paul Olsen

ISBN 1-57748-158-5

Published by Barbour Publishing, Inc., P.O. Box 719, Uhrichsville, Ohio 44683
http://www.barbourbooks.com

Member of the
Evangelical Christian
Publishers Association

Printed in the United States of America.

Cover illustration by Matthew Archambault.
Inside illustrations by Adam Wallenta.

Chapter 1
Mysterious Visitors

Boston, December 16, 1773

"OOF!"

Thirteen-year-old Stephen Lankford braced against the crowd that dragged him and his cousin Anna Allerton along. Whistles and yells from merchants, craftsmen, and seamen filled the early night air.

"A Boston tea party tonight!" called a large man beside him. From the smell of him, Stephen guessed he was one of Boston's many fishermen.

Stephen struggled to keep his footing on the slippery wet stones of Boston's Milk Street. Anna hung onto his arm, making it even harder to keep from falling.

Thousands of people filled the streets. Stephen had never seen such a crowd in Boston! Stephen and Anna had no choice but to go the same way as everyone else. His heart beat like crazy beneath his wool shirt. He'd wondered for weeks what would happen tonight, and now he was about to find out!

"Where's everyone going?" Anna had to yell to be heard. She was shorter than Stephen. The gray wool cloak hood hiding her blond curls came just above his shoulder.

"To Griffin Wharf at Boston Harbor," he called back. "The tea ships are there."

"Are the people going to hurt the crews? Will they sink the ships?"

Fear clumped in his chest like a rock. "I don't think so. People aren't carrying weapons or sticks or stones."

When they reached Griffin Wharf, Stephen had to step quickly to keep from tripping on the slippery wooden planks and huge coils of rope. Beneath them, water lapped at the tall wooden poles that held up the dock.

The people filled the wharf to the very end. Judging by the light from tin and wooden lanterns and long wooden torches people carried, Stephen guessed the next wharf was just as crowded.

The *Dartmouth* rose high above them. It tugged at the thick ropes tying it to the pier. It was one of three ships carrying tea. The other two tea ships were anchored nearby.

"The ships look like dragons, don't they?" Anna giggled.

Stephen looked at the three ships, dark outlines against the darker sky of early evening. With their sails rolled up, the ships' straight pine masts stood like tall, leafless trees.

Will the ships still be here in the morning? Stephen wondered. *Will the tea?*

At least the rain had stopped. The December chill crept through Griffin Wharf's wet wooden planks, up through the soles of his shoes with their pewter buckles, through the three layers of itchy wool socks, through the wool breeches that buckled below his knees, and right into his bones.

He shivered, yanked his wide-brimmed hat farther down over his shoulder-length brown hair, and wrapped his heavy wool cloak closer about him.

It's not only the cold that makes me shiver, he thought. *It's fear.* Fear for Boston. Fear of the unknown. Fear for his older brother William's life.

The fear had been crawling inside him ever since that day two weeks ago at their father's print shop. That was when William had told him what might happen and had asked Stephen to help.

They'd been printing handbills, or posters, for the Sons of Liberty. Stephen didn't mind helping, but he much preferred working with his uncle, Dr. Cuyler Allerton.

Will's eyes, as brown as Stephen's, had flashed with excitement. He'd leaned across the huge printing press and told him the plan in a loud whisper. "The law says the *Dartmouth* has to either leave Boston December sixteenth or unload its tea by then."

"I know." Stephen was hanging up copies of the paper, fresh from the press, to dry. "They've only fourteen days left."

"Mark my words, the tea won't be unloaded or sold here."

Stephen frowned. William was twenty-two, nine years older than Stephen. Still, what could he or the other men do? "I don't understand."

Will spoke quickly, excitedly. "If the ships are unloaded here, we Patriots will do it ourselves. It will take lots of hands. We need men and boys to help who aren't well known in town. Boys who can be trusted not to tell what they do that night—not before and not after. You're a Patriot, Stephen, and I'd trust you with my life."

Pride flooded Stephen at his brother's words. "I'm a Patriot, all right, and I'll keep your secret."

His Dr. Cuyler and cousin Anna would call him a rebel, but he liked Patriot better. Rebel sounded like an enemy of King George III. Patriot sounded like a loyal British citizen, and that's what Stephen was.

Will grinned. "Then you'll help?"

"I don't know. How are you going to unload the tea?"

"We're going to throw the tea into the harbor."

Stephen's heart thumped as loud as his feet when he ran across the wooden planks on the docks. "You're going to ruin it?"

Will nodded once, sharply.

"But. . .but that's like stealing!" Stephen's chest hurt from the deep breaths he was taking. Surely his brother wouldn't steal, even to keep the tea out of Boston!

"We'll only do it if we have to. We're trying to get the governor to send the ships away with the tea. If he does, we won't have to toss the tea overboard."

"What if the governor has you arrested for dumping the tea?"

"That's why we need boys that most adults in town won't

know. Lots of boys your age are helping. Are you with us?"

Stephen swallowed. "I can't. It's too much like stealing."

Would Will think he was a fraidycat? He and Will looked alike and they were Patriots, but those were the only ways they were the same. Will was always doing exciting things. Stephen was quiet, serious. He thought things through carefully before making decisions. Still, Stephen liked Will more than anyone.

"You have to do what you believe is right," Will said.

Stephen let out his breath with relief.

"But," Will continued, "I have to do what I believe is right, too. I know you won't tell anyone what I've told you."

He hadn't told anyone Will's secret. Not even Anna, and he and Anna shared everything. She was easy to talk to. She always listened carefully and never laughed at him.

Anna's tug at his coat sleeve brought Stephen's thoughts back to the cold, damp wharf. "Let's go home."

"We'll never make it through this crowd."

Anna and her family were Loyalists. Loyalists thought the Patriots should do as Parliament and the king said, even if what they said was wrong. He knew she wouldn't want to get Will in trouble, but if she knew Will's secret, she might think it was her duty to tell the British admiral. Then Will's friends would be in trouble.

"If only the governor had let the *Dartmouth* leave tonight with her tea, everything would have been fine," Stephen whispered through chattering teeth.

"Why are people making such a fuss about the tea?" Anna asked. "The tax on it is small, and people like tea."

Stephen had heard people talk about the tea in his father's print shop many times. "In Britain, Parliament passed the tea tax law. Older laws say only people who serve us can pass laws taxing us. No one in Parliament serves the Americans."

Anna's gray wool cloak lifted as she shrugged her shoulders. "Taxation without representation. People say that all the time. But the king chose representatives for the American colonies."

"Those men vote the way the king wants, or they lose their jobs. If we elected them, they'd have to vote the way we want."

"Parliament has a right to make laws, even if Americans don't like them." Anna's pointed chin jutted out.

The crowd grew suddenly still. Stephen looked around. What was happening? Anna stretched onto her tiptoes, trying to see above the people. "I hate being short!"

The crowd opened to let a few raggedly dressed boys and men through.

Anna grabbed his arm. "Indians!"

The newcomers were pretending to be Indians, but Stephen thought anyone could tell they weren't. He could smell the grease and soot they'd used to darken their faces. Swipes of paint brightened some noses. Knit caps hid hair. Feathers were stuck in a few caps. Blankets draped over shoulders.

It was what they carried that made Stephen's heart beat faster: metal things that glittered in the light from the torches and lanterns. "Axes!" Anna whispered. "What are they going to do with them?"

No one answered her.

As more "Indians" came, people pressed even closer together to give them room. Stephen thought there must be over one hundred of them.

One of the ragged, smelly young men bumped against Stephen. He glanced up. The man winked, then passed on to join the others.

Stephen stared after him. William!

Chapter 2
A Wild Tea Party

Stephen glanced at Anna and let out a sigh of relief. She hadn't noticed one of the strangers was her cousin.

Will was helping the "Indians" pull one of the other two tea ships up to the wharf. Fear made Stephen's stomach feel like it was wrapped around itself as tightly as the thick ropes tying the ships to the wharf were coiled. What was going to happen? Would Will and the other Patriots dare go through with their plan?

In the moonlight, he could see the harbor was filled with

every size and kind of ship and boat, just as it had been all his life. Somewhere out there in the dark harbor, British soldiers were stationed at the fort on Castle Island.

Warships were in the harbor, too. He could see the lanterns on the British man-of-war that bounced only a quarter-mile away. All Boston knew the governor had ordered the ships and fort to fire their cannons on the tea ships if they left the harbor with the tea on board.

Anna yanked on his sleeve again. "Do you think the men-of-war will fire their cannons at these Indians?"

"Of course not. They might hurt innocent people." He didn't tell her he was worried the men-of-war might send small boats of marines to stop Will and the others.

"Who are these Indians?" Anna whispered.

"Who can tell under their disguises?" Stephen didn't want to lie to Anna, and he couldn't tell her Will was one of them.

Anna crossed her arms. "I'll bet it's those Sons of Liberty. Sons of Trouble, Papa calls them. They're nothing but trouble-makers, always stirring up the good British citizens in Boston."

Stephen didn't answer. She was probably right about the Sons of Liberty planning this. He wouldn't call them trouble-makers, but they did talk about a lot of things they believed the king and Parliament were doing wrong. Will was a Son of Liberty.

Stephen studied the "Indians." Many looked like they might be about his age. Were any his friends?

Five more joined the group. A man who acted like a leader greeted them by saying, "Me know you." The voice sounded familiar. The five repeated the three words. Stephen guessed it was a sign, a way the "Indians" would know there wasn't a spy in the group.

The moonlight rested on the man's face. Stephen squinted at him. Was that Paul Revere, the silversmith who stopped at the printing shop to talk with Will so often? Surely not. Will had said they wanted people who wouldn't be recognized. Lots of people knew Mr. Revere. Still, the man's voice had sounded like Mr. Revere's.

The "Indians" quietly boarded the three tea ships. Standing close to the *Dartmouth,* Stephen heard someone on deck say, "We no hurt your ship, Captain, only the tea. Please bring lanterns."

Was the speaker afraid someone would recognize his voice if he spoke normally? Stephen wondered. The Indians who still lived anywhere near Boston didn't speak English like that.

In a few minutes, lanterns shined on the three ships' decks. Then came whack! whack! whack!—the sound of axes chopping open wooden chests. In the light from the lanterns and the moon, Stephen and the crowd watched smashed boxes drop over the ships' sides.

Anna gasped. "They are throwing the tea into the water! Where are the constables, or the night watchmen, or the marines?"

"I guess they can't get through the crowd. Maybe they don't know what's happening."

"These people are no better than thieves! Why doesn't someone stop them?"

"No one wants trouble, Anna. They just want the tea unloaded tonight like the law says it must be."

"The law doesn't mean it's to be unloaded this way, and you know it!"

Stephen shifted his feet uncomfortably. Anna was right.

What was happening was illegal. Still, the Patriots had tried to have it sent legally away from Boston first.

Stephen was surprised to see both Loyalists and Patriots watching quietly. Did the Loyalists think, like the Patriots, that destroying the tea was the only thing left to do?

He didn't see any of the Patriot leaders in the crowd. Sam Adams, John Hancock, Josiah Quincy, and Dr. Warren had all been at the town meeting at Old South earlier. Was it too dangerous for them to be seen here?

It went on for three hours: the whack of axes, the sound of canvas tearing—Stephen guessed that was the bags inside the wooden chests, bags meant to keep the tea dry if the chests got wet. The bags wouldn't help now.

Splintered chests splashed as they landed alongside the ships. The wooden chests bobbed in the moonlight. Spilled tea drifted like seaweed on top of the dark water. He could smell the tea over the strong smell of sea and fish.

Stephen's legs grew tired. He knew Anna's must be tired, too, for she leaned against him. But he never thought of leaving. No one else left, either.

For a while, Stephen watched nervously for boats of marines to come from the men-of-war. They never came.

When all the tea had been dumped, the "Indians" finally left the ships. They lined up, four in a row. *Just like soldiers,* Stephen thought, chuckling. They rested their axes on their shoulders the same way soldiers rested their rifles. Someone played a tune on a fife.

The tea destroyers marched down the wharf toward town. Stephen spotted Will. He hurried to get near him, keeping a tight hold on Anna's hand so they wouldn't lose each other.

Stephen grinned as he kept up with the men, humming the

cheerful tune the fife played. Now that everything was over, he wished he'd joined Will and the boys his age. It couldn't have been so bad after all, since even the Loyalists and British marines hadn't tried to stop it. Surely no one would be arrested. It would have been exciting to be part of it.

The marching men reached the head of Griffin Wharf, where buildings lined the street at the edge of the harbor. Wood squeaked against wood as a window opened. Stephen looked up just in time to see a man shove his head out the window above them. Admiral Montague of the British marines! He'd watched the whole thing!

Stephen stopped in his tracks so fast that the man behind him ran right into him. Stephen didn't even notice.

"Well, boys," the admiral said, "you've had a nice night for your Indian caper, haven't you? But mind, you have got to pay the fiddler yet."

One of the "Indians" made a smart reply. The admiral slammed the window closed.

The men started marching again. Stephen's thoughts spun as he followed. He wasn't humming now. The admiral's words made him sick to his stomach.

How would the admiral make Will and the tea raiders "pay the fiddler"?

"We'd best get home, Stephen," Anna said.

"I didn't realize it was so late," Stephen said as they threaded their way through the crowded streets toward Anna's house. "It must be after nine o'clock. I'll walk you home. You shouldn't be on the streets alone this late."

"Mother will be furious I'm still out."

Anna was right. They were barely through the front door when Anna's mother met them in the hallway. Like Anna,

Aunt Abigail was short with blond hair and blue eyes, but she wasn't slender like Anna.

"Where have you been, young lady?" Aunt Abigail's eyes flashed as she faced them.

"We were at the meeting at Old South Meetinghouse. You said I could go, remember?"

"That was early this afternoon. You know you're to be home before dark. Your father is out searching the streets for you."

"But Mother, you can't imagine what happened!"

"I've been imagining all kinds of dreadful things happening to you."

"I've been with her the whole time, Aunt Abigail," Stephen spoke up.

"Humph! There are things a boy of thirteen like yourself can't protect her from." Aunt Abigail wrapped her shawl closer about her shoulders. "I shouldn't have allowed you out of the house today at all, Anna. With the Patriots in such a vile mood over the tea ships and the crowds in the streets— why, I wouldn't be surprised if we ended up with another Boston Massacre."

"Oh, no, Mama!" Anna said eagerly. "The British marines didn't do anything to stop the Indians!"

"Indians?" Aunt Abigail's hand flew to her throat.

"Not true Indians," Anna assured her quickly.

Mrs. Allerton shook her head. "I don't know what you are talking about, child. Stephen you'd best get home. Take a lantern with you. Honestly, out on the streets without even a lantern, among the angry crowds. You both should have known better."

"Yes, Aunt Abigail," Stephen murmured, moving past her

into the parlor to light the candle for the lantern at the fireplace.

"Don't think you're going to get by without being punished for this," Aunt Abigail was saying to Anna as Stephen slipped out the door.

"But let me tell you about the tea and the Indians," he heard Anna say as the door closed.

He knew Aunt Abigail had been worried about Anna, but he didn't understand why being worried always made parents angry. He dreaded going home. His parents would be just as angry as Aunt Abigail. Of course, he and Anna deserved to be punished. They knew better than to stay out so late.

Things are even worse than at Anna's, he thought a few minutes later in front of the parlor fireplace.

At least Anna didn't have a room full of people listening to her mother bawl her out. Stephen fidgeted, well aware of his older sisters Lydia, age fifteen, and Kathleen, age twenty, as well as William's wife, Eliza, keeping their gazes on their fancy needlework while his mother spoke. William and Eliza's six-month-old baby, Paul, slept in a wooden cradle beside the hearth.

Stephen's mother was tall and lean like her brother, Anna's father. She had red hair and freckles like her Irish mother. Right now her green eyes were stormy.

"I'm sorry, Mother," Stephen said, "but we just forgot about the time. We wanted to see what happened, and the crowd was so thick—"

The sound of the back door closing interrupted him. A minute later, a tall figure moved into the shadows at the edge of the parlor.

The women gasped.

"Who. . .who are you?" Mrs. Lankford asked.

The figure stepped into the candlelight, a grin splitting his darkened face. "It's me, Mother."

"William! Why are you dressed like that? You smell like tea leaves!"

A moment later Father came into the parlor. He'd been in the crowd at Old South and Griffin Wharf, but there had been so many people that Stephen hadn't seen him.

Stephen's lateness was forgotten as Will told the women about the tea party. Ever since the Boston Massacre, Stephen's father and mother had become more sympathetic toward the Patriot cause. Now everyone clapped and laughed at Will's story.

Will slipped off a leather shoe and shook it. "Think some of the tea sifted into my shoes." He dumped the tea onto the fire.

Mother laughed. "Abigail would hate to see that. She does love her English tea." She slipped an arm around Stephen's shoulders. "I'm proud you and your father stand up for Englishmen's rights, Will, but I'm glad you didn't ask Stephen to join the other boys tonight. He's so young."

Stephen squirmed away from his mother's arm. "Mother, I'm thirteen!"

"Yes, still a boy."

It didn't matter how old he was, he'd always be the baby of the family!

"Won't be a boy much longer," Will said, winking at him.

Stephen relaxed. Will didn't think he was too young to help the Patriots. Stephen was tempted to tell his mother that Will *had* asked him to help with the tea party. He decided he'd best not. He was already in trouble for being out late.

"No one here must ever mention that Will was involved with the tea party," Father warned. "The marines and constables didn't arrest anyone tonight, but we don't know what might happen later."

Stephen noticed he didn't tell the women about the admiral's warning: "You have got to pay the fiddler yet."

CHAPTER 3

What Happened to Liberty?

"King George is making Boston 'pay the fiddler' now," Stephen said to Anna early in June.

"He's making all Boston pay, not just those awful men who threw the tea overboard." Anna's mouth bent in a pout.

The peal of bells drifted over the water. All the churches in Boston had been ringing their bells for hours. Everyone said it was the worst day in Boston's history.

So many months had passed since the tea party that Stephen

had hoped the king had forgotten about it. He hadn't. Finally a ship came from England carrying the Boston Port Bill. The bill was a law passed by Parliament. It said that until Boston paid for the tea it dumped into the harbor, Boston's port would be closed.

From where they stood on Long Wharf, which ran half a mile into Boston Harbor, Stephen could see the British man-of-war anchored between Long Wharf and Hancock's Wharf. In all, there were nine men-of-war guarding the harbor from entering ships. There were no other ships in the harbor. The warships wouldn't let small boats, barges, or ferries approach Boston by harbor or river. A small boat couldn't be rowed from one dock to another.

Boston was built on a peninsula. It was almost an island. Only a narrow piece of land, called the Neck, connected it to the rest of Massachusetts. With the harbor closed, the Neck was the only way in or out of town.

At least no one had been arrested for the tea party, Stephen thought. Because no one knew for certain who more than a couple of the tea partyers were—and wouldn't tell if they did—no one had been arrested. The day after the tea party, Paul Revere had left for Philadelphia and New York to let people there know what had happened. Sons of Liberty in those cities had sent back word that they thought Boston had done the right thing.

Hardly anyone was working. People wandered about town, angry, unable to believe what was happening. A soft salt breeze cooled the summer day but did nothing to cool people's tempers.

Stephen and Anna had joined their families in a prayer service at church before coming to the wharf. Loyalists,

Patriots, and people who hadn't chosen sides had been there. Everyone was afraid the port closing would leave people without jobs.

The Allertons and Lankfords, as well as several other families that had been at the prayer service, looked out at the changes in the harbor. Anna shoved a blond curl behind her ear, out of the breeze's way. "I've never seen the wharf so quiet. There's none of the usual bustle of unloading and loading ships and clerks running about with their ledgers. And none of Uncle Ethan's merchant ships are in the harbor."

Their uncle Ethan owned merchant ships. The king thought when Boston's port closed, the other towns would jump at the chance to take business away from Boston. Instead they'd offered to help Boston. Uncle Ethan was in Salem arranging for his ships to land at Salem's port. His merchandise would have to be shipped over land, which would cost more money and make business more difficult, but it would keep business from stopping altogether.

"Only our enemies' ships are in our harbor," Stephen's father said.

Sparks flew from Dr. Cuyler's eyes. "The British fleet isn't our enemy. Boston is part of England."

Father's brown eyes grew cold. "Since when does England point cannons at its own people?"

"Since Boston's people threw someone else's tea into the harbor. Even Ben Franklin sent word from London that the tea party was illegal. He thinks Boston should pay for the tea."

"Boston's citizens would sooner starve."

"I don't think so. There are lots of Loyalists in town. We don't want to lose business because of what the tea partyers did. With the port closed, it won't take long for the rest of

Boston to come to its senses and pay for the tea."

"Never!"

Dr. Cuyler waved an arm toward the shops, counting-houses, and warehouses on the wharf. "Can't you see these buildings are closed and their windows shuttered? The men are without work. People won't be able to buy food or clothing or your newspapers. How are you going to run your print shop?"

"I've bought a good supply of paper and ink," Father answered. "I agree things will be rough if people don't have money to buy newspapers or place ads. There will be news the people need to know, and I aim to print it. I'll say things with fewer words and use less paper."

"And when you run out of ink?" Dr. Cuyler asked. Stephen waited for his father's answer. British law said people in America had to buy all their ink from England.

Father crossed his arms. "Then Will and I will learn to make it ourselves."

Stephen stared at his father. Could they do that?

"Boston will get by," Father continued. "Sons of Liberty in New York and Philadelphia have promised to help us."

"How?" Dr. Cuyler waved a hand scornfully. "With brave words? The other colonies don't care about us. Do you think they'll give Boston fuel, food, and other supplies?"

Stephen remembered the picture of the snake his father had printed in the newspaper the previous week. Ben Franklin had drawn it many years ago. The snake was in pieces, each piece representing a different colony. The pieces weren't joined together because the colonies always argued among themselves instead of working together. Beneath the picture Mr. Franklin had written "Join or Die." He'd said that if the colonies didn't work together, they would die.

Was Dr. Cuyler right? Stephen wondered. Wouldn't the other colonies help Boston?

"Remember what I printed in yesterday's paper?" Stephen's father asked. "Colonel George Washington threatened to raise one thousand men and force the British troops from Boston."

"You wish to see fighting in our streets?" Dr. Cuyler's face was red from fury.

"No, but I don't wish to give up our rights as English citizens, either, just to keep peace."

Anna leaned close to whisper, "Our fathers haven't stopped fighting in years. Why can't they be friendly like us? You're a Patriot and I'm a Loyalist, but we don't argue about it."

Dr. Cuyler turned to Stephen and Anna. "We'd best get back to the apothecary. A doctor's work doesn't stop because people can't pay him. There may be more work than ever for you, Stephen. My other apprentice, Johnny, left Boston with his family. You'll have to take over his duties, too. You can start by weeding the medicine herb garden."

Dr. Cuyler's long legs set a brisk pace. Short Anna in her long skirt and petticoat couldn't keep up, so Stephen matched his steps to hers. "I didn't know Johnny was leaving."

Anna lifted her skirts so they wouldn't be soiled by the puddle they were passing. "He and his family went to Salem. Johnny's father is looking for a job there."

Stephen nodded. Johnny's father was a carpenter who worked in the shipyards. The Port Bill put him out of work.

He'd miss Johnny, Stephen thought. Johnny wanted to be a doctor more than anything. What if he never had the chance again? Stephen's chest ached for him. He couldn't bear it if his own father made him give up his chance to be a doctor.

Many houses they passed were empty. Shops were empty

and dark, too. They gave Stephen an eerie feeling. Families leaving town passed them with carts and arms piled high with belongings.

Anna's eyebrows scrunched together. "Johnny's father said the people who stay in Boston are going to starve. Do you think we're going to st. . .starve?"

Stephen could see the fear in her blue eyes. "Of course not. Didn't you hear Father say the other colonies will help us?"

But would they? Goose bumps ran up his arms. Who was right, Dr. Cuyler or his father?

Hours later at the apothecary, Stephen held a small marble bowl in one hand and a marble pestle in the other, grinding soft yellow primrose flower petals into powder. Dr. Cuyler wanted them for a patient. Primrose would help the woman's painful hands. The flower's gentle smell filled the air.

The woman had barely left before off-key singing came through the open door:

"Rally, Mohawks! Bring out your axes,
and tell King George we'll pay no taxes on his
foreign tea!"

The doctor grunted. "You'd think people would be sick of that song about the tea party."

Stephen grinned. He liked the song, but it did get under the skin of Loyalists like Dr. Cuyler.

He took his journal from the open shelves, where he kept it handy. The shelves were filled with white jars. Blue letters told what herbs each held. Stephen liked the way the apothecary always smelled of dried flowers and herbs. Drawers below the shelves held roots and barks for medicines and curved saws for surgery.

His quill pen's tip scratched across the page as he wrote down what Dr. Cuyler, as Stephen called his uncle in the shop, had told the woman about the primrose. Stephen had been an apprentice for almost three years now.

Dr. Cuyler smiled down at him. "I'm glad you like to learn. You're the best apprentice I've ever had."

Stephen's cheeks warmed with pride. "I don't want to forget how to treat all the different sicknesses when I'm a doctor."

"You'll have books to help you remember, like this new one you bought at Henry Knox's bookshop down the street." The doctor lifted a thick book bound in brown leather with gold letters.

"I. . .I want to get a degree from a medical school, too." Stephen held his breath. It was his greatest dream to get a university degree. He'd never told anyone but Anna.

Dr. Cuyler nodded. "You don't need to go to a university to be a doctor. Most doctors learn only through apprenticeship and reading, as you're learning."

"I know, sir, but I want to be the best doctor possible. I want to know everything I can to help my patients."

"Have you decided which university you want to go to?"

"Either Philadelphia or King's College in New York. They're the only medical schools in the American colonies."

Crash!

Stephen and Dr. Cuyler spun toward the door. Anna leaned against it. Wrapped in her apron, she carried a small tan dog with a black nose and a black tip on its long, skinny tail.

"Liberty!" Stephen cried. "What happened to my dog?"

CHAPTER 4

Will Boston Starve?

The lilac dress Anna had worn at the wharf earlier was covered with dirt. The ties of her white linen scarf had slid up under one ear. Her friend Sara stood beside her.

"Put Liberty on the counter," Dr. Cuyler said.

Stephen could see she laid the dog down gently, but Liberty still whimpered. He ran a hand lightly over the dog's short fur. His heart ached for his little friend. "It's okay, boy."

"It's his right front leg." Anna was still trying to catch her breath. "He can't walk on it."

Dr. Cuyler took the leg carefully between his hands. Liberty yelped and tried to sit up. Stephen put his hands on both sides of Liberty's head. "Shhh, Liberty."

While Dr. Cuyler ran his fingers lightly over the rest of Liberty's body, looking for other injuries, Stephen looked at Anna. "What happened? Was he hit by a carriage?"

Tears pooled in Anna's blue eyes, but they couldn't hide the anger that flashed there. "No. It was some mean Loyalist boys. When the boys heard me call him Liberty, they said he was a nasty Patriot dog. They threw stones at him!"

Anger flashed through Stephen. How could anyone be so cruel?

"His leg is broken," Dr. Cuyler said.

"I'll set it." Stephen glanced up at the doctor. "I mean, if you don't mind, sir."

"You certainly know how to handle a broken leg by now. I'll get some bandages and wood for a splint." He started for the small room at the back where wood was stored.

"You should have seen Anna," Sara's blue eyes sparkled above her freckled nose. Her dark brown hair waved over her shoulders. "She yelled at the boys to stop. They called her awful names and kept throwing stones at poor Liberty. Anna ran into the middle of them and picked up Liberty in her apron. I tried to stop her. I was afraid the stones would hurt her."

Dr. Cuyler whirled around. He grabbed his daughter's shoulders. "Were you hurt?"

Anna winced. "Not much." She rubbed a dirty spot at the top of one arm. "I think I might have a black and blue spot here."

"A rock hit her on the head, too," Sara offered eagerly.

Anna scowled at her. Dr. Cuyler pushed her scarf back.

"Anna, there's a lump here as large as a goose egg!"

She squirmed under her father's gaze. "Well, I haven't a broken leg like Liberty."

"You could have been hurt badly," Dr. Cuyler said. "What if a rock had hit you in the face?"

She shrugged. "It didn't. Anyway, I couldn't let them keep hurting Liberty!"

Dr. Cuyler shook his head. "I don't know whether to punish you or praise you."

"It's those stupid Loyalist boys who should be punished," Sara stormed. "Just shows how awful Loyalists are."

Anna rolled her eyes and propped her hands on her hips. "*My* family are Loyalists, remember?"

"I forgot."

Stephen smiled at Sara's blush.

Dr. Cuyler started back toward the wood room. "We'd best set Liberty's leg. Go clean up before your mother sees you, Anna."

Stephen cleared his throat. "Anna, thank you. You're a good friend and a brave one."

Sara grinned. "Even if you are a Loyalist."

Stephen knew Sara and her family were strong Patriots. Her father was even more outspoken about Englishmen's rights than his father and William.

Anna smiled at Stephen and petted Liberty's head. "I'm just glad Liberty wasn't hurt any worse."

Liberty tried to lick her hand. Stephen knew how he felt. He would have hugged Anna if there weren't anyone around to see.

A month later, shades of pink and orange cast by the rising

sun were fading from the sky over Boston's streets and harbor as Stephen, Kathleen, and Anna hurried down the cobbled, narrow street toward the common. Two and three-story brick houses hugged the street's edge on either side of them. The homes and shops were built so close their walls touched. Smoke from breakfast fires and craftsmen's fires filled the air.

Stephen leaped into a nearby doorway to let a farmer and his creaking, two-wheeled cart pass. He grinned. "Look at the turkey." The bird sat in the cart atop a basket of turnips. It turned its head this way and that and gobbled constantly. "At least farmers can still get into Boston over the Neck to sell their food, even if nothing can come by boat or ferry."

Anna's smile died. "Farmers come to the market, but people aren't buying much. People don't have much money. Sara's father is a carpenter. He hasn't had any work since the harbor closed."

Many of Anna's father's patients hadn't paid the doctor, either, Stephen remembered. Some people made less money in a month than they used to make in a day.

"Many farmers sell most of their vegetables, flour, and meat to the soldiers and marines," Kathleen said. "The redcoats won't starve. Britain sends ships with food for them."

Anna sighed. "Father says things will get worse after harvest is over."

"Harvest is months away," Stephen said. "Surely the blockade will be over by then."

Anna's blue eyes sparkled with hope. "Do you think so?"

"I haven't heard anyone say so," he admitted. "Still, I can't believe the British troops would let people starve. Even some of the Patriots are friendly with the soldiers. Some of the soldiers are courting Boston girls. Why, I've even heard that Lieutenant Colonel Percy breakfasts every day with John Hancock. There's no stronger Patriot than Mr. Hancock! Could the soldiers hurt the townspeople when they are so friendly with us?"

"I hope you're right." Anna sighed.

Kathleen rested her arm along Anna's shoulders and smiled. "Our heavenly Father will look out for us, you'll see."

"I hope He looks out for us better than the other colonies," Anna said. "They promised to help us, but they haven't yet."

Fear squiggled down Stephen's spine. Maybe Dr. Cuyler was right, and the other colonies weren't going to help Boston.

Before they reached the common, they heard the silver bugles calling the redcoats to drill. The day after the harbor was closed, a regiment of British troops had set up camp on the common. Now four regiments were camped there and two groups of artillery with cannons. Cannons on the common, threatening Boston's own people! In the harbor, men-of-war pointed more cannons at the town. A year ago, Stephen would never have thought such a thing could happen.

Still, part of him couldn't help but find it exciting to have the streets, shops, and common filled with soldiers in the bright red uniforms that made people call them "lobsterbacks" and "redcoats." When he watched them drill, a thrill ran through him. He didn't tell anyone. He was ashamed to feel that way.

Tents and red-and-white uniforms splashed color across the common's grassy slopes. Soldiers were smothering the fires where they'd cooked their breakfast. Stephen could still smell the meat and eggs they'd cooked. Some soldiers were readying horses for the officers. Others were grabbing muskets from where they'd been stacked in a circle and rushing to line up for drill. Men and boys from Boston stood in groups, watching. With the port closed, many had time to watch instead of work.

Stephen stopped near a bay-colored horse with a black mane and tail. He ran a hand over the horse's shoulder. It turned his head and sniffed Stephen's hand.

"What are you looking at, lad?"

Stephen's head jerked toward the tall officer beside the horse. Like all officers, he wore a powdered white wig that curled tightly at his ears and tied in a club in back. His black eyebrows showed his hair's true color.

Stephen swallowed the lump in his throat. "I. . .I was just looking at the fine horse, sir."

"Maybe you were thinking of stealing her."

"No, sir! I wouldn't!"

The officer crossed his arms and looked Stephen up and down. "I suppose you're a Patriot rebel brat."

Stephen's hand balled into a fist. "I'm a—" he stopped short. He wanted to say he was a Patriot and proud of it. His father and William had warned all the family to be careful what they said around the soldiers. The Patriot leaders didn't want to anger the troops. "I'm an English citizen," he finished, lamely.

The officer snorted. "Not a loyal one, I'll bet."

Kathleen's fists perched on her hips. Long red curls slipped over the shoulder of her yellow muslin gown. "You needn't speak to him that way. Have British officers no manners?"

"It isn't wise for the town's boys to be fooling with an officer's horse, miss." The officer stared boldly at her.

"Is there a problem here, Lieutenant Rand?" A calm, sure voice spoke as another officer stepped up beside him.

Lieutenant Rand straightened. "Just speaking with some of the locals."

"I'm Lieutenant John Andrews." The new officer's friendly, blue-eyed gaze swept over them. "I'm honored to make your acquaintance." Removing his two-cornered black hat, he bowed from the waist. "Have you come to see the troops, lad?"

"No, sir. I brought medicine for the regiment's doctor."

A frown settled above the blue eyes. "That's a strange delivery, isn't it?"

"I'm Stephen Lankford, Dr. Cuyler Allerton's apprentice. This is my sister, Kathleen, and Dr. Cuyler's daughter, Anna. Your regiment's doctor sent a soldier to Dr. Cuyler saying he needed certain herbs. I've brought them for him, but I don't know where to find him."

"The doctor's tent is over there." Lieutenant Andrews pointed to the top of a grassy knoll where a tent was pitched beneath a tall oak. "If I might suggest, it would be best if you young ladies didn't come near the soldiers' camps without a male escort."

Stephen stepped between the officer and Kathleen. "That's why *I'm* with them."

Surprise widened Lieutenant Andrews's eyes. Stephen waited for him to say that Stephen was only a boy. Instead he only nodded and shook hands with Stephen. "Of course. How wise of you." With another bow to Kathleen and Anna, he left.

"He's awfully nice, isn't he?" Anna stared after him.

"He's a British officer. The reason he's in Boston isn't nice at all," Stephen reminded her.

Anna smiled smugly. "Maybe all these soldiers will make Boston pay for the tea."

"Girls!" Stephen exclaimed in disgust and stalked toward the doctor's tent.

When they headed back toward town, the streets were filled with more families piling carts with everything they owned and leaving Boston. Stephen knew they were afraid there'd be fighting with troops in Boston. Many more troops were on their way.

"Stephen!"

Stephen turned to see William running toward them, his tricorn hat in one hand. "Great news!" He stopped beside them, panting and grinning.

"What is it?"

"Rice. South Carolina's sent two hundred barrels of rice. The rice is coming across the Neck now. And Carolina's promised to send eight hundred more barrels." Will whipped his hat in the air. "They're uniting! The colonies are uniting for Boston!"

CHAPTER 5
Signs of War

To the surprise of the Loyalists and redcoats, gifts poured in over the Neck. The other colonies sent rice, meal, flour, rye, bread, codfish, cattle, and money. A farmer from Connecticut brought an entire flock of sheep.

Stephen and Anna's Uncle Ethan was on the town's Gifts Committee, along with some of the colonies' strongest Patriots, Sam and John Adams and Josiah Quincy.

When Uncle Ethan asked Anna to help deliver gifts, she eagerly said yes. It didn't matter whether the people she took the gifts to were Patriots or Loyalists. "No one should go hungry, no matter what he believes," she told Stephen.

"Thanks to the other towns and colonies, no one in Boston *has* gone hungry," Stephen said.

Anna's shoulders sagged beneath her yellow-and-blue calico gown. "If the Patriots would pay for the tea, people wouldn't have to beg the committee for food."

"It's not the Patriots' fault King George is punishing everyone in Boston for what the tea partyers did," Stephen said quietly.

Anna began dusting the shelves with her long-handled feather duster in quick, jerky motions. Stephen sighed. He and Anna argued more and more now, like their fathers.

The men who were out of work were growing angrier every day. They couldn't buy what their families needed and had nothing to do with their time. They fished off the empty, quiet wharves and complained about the king. They were certain the king was wrong and the Patriots were right. People who didn't know whether to be Loyalists or Patriots before the tea party became Patriots.

In order to receive the food that the other colonies had donated, Bostonians had to volunteer for various projects. Streets were paved, buildings were fixed, docks were cleaned, wharves were repaired, and hundreds worked at the brickyard on the Neck.

"It's like the town is having a housecleaning!" Anna joked to Stephen when she came home from making deliveries one day.

On a day in late August, Stephen whistled as he walked home from Dr. Cuyler's. He liked the bustle and sounds of the street: a boy beating a drum while calling out his master's wares, wooden cart and wagon wheels rumbling along the pebbles, horses' hooves marking a lazy beat, the creak of the wooden signs above every shop swinging in the breeze.

If only there weren't redcoats everywhere.

He stopped in the open door of his father's printing shop. Lieutenant Rand was waving a sheet of freshly printed paper and yelling at Stephen's father and Will. "This is treason!" His face was almost as red as his uniform.

Mr. Lankford leaned a hip against the tall wooden printing press and swung his wire-rimmed spectacles in one hand. Stephen wondered how he could be so calm with a British officer screaming at him only a couple feet away. "The handbill only tells what our county leaders said today at their meeting."

Lieutenant Rand threw the handbill down and ground it into the wooden floor planks with the heel of his shiny black boot. "They've all but declared war on England!"

"Lieutenant Rand, what they said is not my problem. With the harbor closed, I'll gladly print items for either Patriots or Loyalists in order to feed my family."

Stephen watched wide-eyed as Lieutenant Rand clutched the hilt of the sword that hung at his side. Surely the lieutenant wouldn't draw his sword on his father! Stephen's heart beat so hard it made his chest hurt.

Lieutenant Rand let go of his sword. His eyes glittered with anger. "Mr. Lankford, be *very* careful what you print from now on."

Stephen stepped quickly from the doorway to get out of Lieutenant Rand's way as the officer left. "Why is he so mad?"

Will grinned. "The Suffolk County leaders drew up this list because of the Port Bill and Intolerable Acts." He handed Stephen a copy of the handbill.

The Intolerable Acts were Boston's latest punishment for

the tea party. Parliament called them Regulatory Acts. Patriots called them Intolerable Acts, because they said no Englishman would tolerate or stand for them.

The Intolerable Acts changed the way Massachusetts was run. Instead of elections, the king and his friends chose people for all the important jobs. Juries were even appointed by the king's friends, so it would be hard for people to get fair trials.

Stephen stood in the doorway where there was enough light to read the list. "Suffolk Resolves" was printed in large letters at the top. The most dangerous thing it said was just what had made Lieutenant Rand so angry: that Massachusetts' army should train and be ready to fight to keep the rights the king and Parliament wanted to take away.

Fear slid through Stephen in an icy wave. "Are the Patriots declaring war on England?"

"No." Will's brown eyes were serious. "But we need to be ready to protect ourselves."

"We could use your help, Stephen," Father said. "Paul Revere is waiting for us to finish these handbills. He'll take them to the Continental Congress meeting in Philadelphia."

Stephen knew the colonies had decided to hold a meeting called the Continental Congress. People from every colony were invited. They wanted to make a plan to convince the king and Parliament to leave Boston alone and give people in America back the rights they used to have.

It was like Will had said months ago, Stephen thought. The king meant to hurt Boston by closing the harbor. Instead the Lord was using Boston's trouble for something good, to get the colonies to work together.

Stephen put on a leather apron to protect his linen shirt and brown cotton breeches. Then the three worked together for hours, taking turns wetting the pieces of paper, inking the type with ink-soaked balls of wool and leather, swinging the large wooden handle to work the press, and hanging up the paper to dry when it came off the press. Before they finished, they had to light candles and lanterns to see.

Stephen didn't usually like working with the printing press, but tonight was different. It felt good to work hard with his father and brother.

Mr. Revere arrived as Will hung up the last handbill. Dark eyes twinkled in his ruddy face. "It looks like you've been helping with the handbills, Stephen. We shall make a Son of Liberty of you yet."

Stephen grinned and felt his night's hard work well paid.

"I wish I could be with you in Philadelphia, Paul, to hear what the Continental Congress thinks of the handbill," Father said, removing his apron.

Will agreed eagerly. "I wonder if they'll dare say they feel as we do about the army."

"You may be sure I'll let you know." Mr. Revere held out a sheet of copper to Stephen's father. "Here's the engraving I promised you."

Father put on his wire glasses. He held the metal near a tin and glass lantern to check the picture the silversmith had carved into the copper. "Perfect. I'll use it in the next copy of the *Boston Observer.*"

Mr. Revere picked up some handbills and started for the door. His boots jingled. Stephen saw his spurs made the sound.

"Are you leaving tonight?" he asked.

He supposed he shouldn't be surprised. Sam Adams had set up a system of post riders to carry news between towns and colonies. It was called the Committees of Correspondence.

Paul Revere often rode for them.

Mr. Revere said, "The congress begins in only nine days. The trip to Philadelphia often takes twice that long. I've a strong horse, but I'll have a hard ride."

Stephen and Will watched from the doorway while Mr. Lankford walked with Paul Revere to his horse, which was tied to a post in front of the shop. Stephen remembered Mr. Revere's copper engraving. "What is the picture he made, Will?"

"It shows how to make saltpeter. If war comes, the Patriots will need saltpeter to make ammunition. We won't be able to buy it from England."

War! The word never went away. A shiver ran through Stephen. "I thought the Patriots didn't want war. I thought we just wanted things back the way they were."

Will nodded. "So we do. We can't always have what we want without a fight, though. We need to be ready, just in case."

Stephen remembered how angry Lieutenant Rand had been earlier that day, how quickly he'd grabbed for his sword. It wouldn't take very much for a few angry men on either side to start a fight like the Boston Massacre four years ago.

Then the people of Boston had been able to make peace again. This time if there was a riot and one side began shooting, would the people be able to keep peace, or would there be war?

CHAPTER 6
A Spy

Stephen, Anna, and Liberty hurried along the road to the Neck on a cool September day. Sara's father was helping build a wall there for General Gage, and they wanted to see it. With the harbor closed, there wasn't much else to watch in Boston these days, except soldiers.

A family that looked tired after walking a long way scuffed along carrying bundles and leaning on walking sticks. They were headed toward Boston.

"Another Loyalist family," Anna said. "If we didn't live in Boston, my family might have been forced to leave our home as well."

Stephen could hear the anger and pain in her voice. Patriots in towns other than Boston were mad at the Loyalists for the punishments King George and Parliament were forcing on Boston. Patriots were threatening Loyalists, chasing them from their homes. The Loyalists had nowhere to go but Boston. "I guess the Loyalists know the redcoats here will keep them safe. How are things going with the Loyalist family from Concord that moved into your house last week?"

"I *hate* sharing our home with them." Anna kicked at a stone and almost tripped over the petticoat beneath her pink skirt. "Esther—she's my age—shares my bed. She won't play with Sara because Sara is a Patriot. Sara is furious."

"Maybe she thinks you feel the same way as Esther."

"I couldn't! Sara's my best friend. She's much nicer than Esther. There's lots more work with Esther's family, too."

"Doesn't Esther's mother tell her to help with the chores?"

"Esther and her mother spend all their time saying how terrible the Patriots are and eating our food. Today Esther complained that we hadn't more sweets. With the price of sugar and molasses, we can't afford many sweets."

"She sounds spoiled."

"Mother says not to speak badly of her." Anna sighed. "It must be awful to be forced out of their home. They only had time to pack a few clothes. I truly am sorry for her."

They reached a small rise in the road as she finished talking.

Soldiers and workmen covered the Neck in front of them.

Some were working, others watched. A few days after Paul Revere left for Philadelphia, General Gage had ordered a wall built all the way across the Neck. He called it fortifications because the wall protected the town like the wall of a fort.

It was a cool day, but sweat slid down Stephen's spine. The townspeople couldn't leave Boston by water because of the warships. Now they wouldn't be able to leave by the only road out of Boston if General Gage decided they shouldn't. Seeing the wall and cannons made Stephen feel like a prisoner in his own town.

Townsmen were teasing the soldiers. "Can't ye build any better than that?" called one man. "Your wall is no stronger than a beaver dam!" yelled another. "That wall won't protect you. A group of Patriots could blow it down!" called a boy about Stephen's age.

Some soldiers ignored them. Others yelled nasty comments back at them. But the townspeople knew the officers wouldn't let the soldiers harm them.

Stephen and Anna sat down beneath an oak tree to watch. Workers hauled bricks in two-wheeled wooden carts. Others laid the bricks to make the wall. Sweat glistened off the men's faces. Their shirts were wet with sweat. Officers yelled orders. In the middle of it all, people and carts and donations filed over the Neck along the road into and out of Boston.

Anna's stomach growled. She put a hand over her apron that protected her dress and laughed, embarrassed.

Stephen smiled. "Seems everyone's always hungry these days. Thanks to the gifts at least no one's starving." He pulled two small green apples from his breeches pockets and handed her one. The breeches used to belong to William, as had his patched white shirt. Stephen had grown so much during the last year that his own clothes no longer fit. "These are from our apple tree."

Stephen watched a boy a couple years older than him push a cart filled with bricks. The boy's red hair was tied back in a club with a piece of leather. He wore a blue farmer's smock that came almost to his knees over his homespun breeches and a black hat with a floppy brim. While Stephen watched, one of the wheels struck a large rock and started to tip.

"Watch out!" Stephen jumped up and darted forward.

The boy struggled with the cart's wooden handles, trying to keep the load upright. Before Stephen could reach him, the bricks shifted to one side. The cart tipped. Hard clay bricks poured out on top of the boy.

Stephen dropped to his knees and frantically pushed bricks off the boy. The lad groaned, trying to sit up.

Other men hurried to help Stephen free him. As the bricks were cleared, Stephen fought back a wave of panic at the sight of the boy's leg. The bricks had torn away the knee-high stocking. He could see how badly the leg was hurt.

"We'll have to stop the bleeding." He glanced about quickly, then turned to one of the men beside him. "I'm a doctor's apprentice. Is there any drinking water about?"

"I'll get some." The man scurried to get the bucket.

Stephen looked up at Anna, who was staring down at the boy's leg, wide-eyed. "Give me your apron."

She unpinned the part of the apron that covered the top of her dress, then untied the bow in back. When she handed it to him, he ripped off the square that made up the top of the apron. He heard Anna gasp, but she didn't say anything. He tore the apron's ties off, then tore the rest of the apron in half.

The workman returned with the leather water bucket, panting slightly and sloshing water onto the ground in his haste.

The boy clutched Stephen's arm. "What. . .what are yuh goin' to do?" His face was pale as a clamshell and covered with sweat. His hat had fallen off, and his red hair was as damp as his face. Green eyes, huge and frightened, stared up at Stephen.

Stephen smiled, trying to look brave. "I'm going to clean your leg and stop the bleeding so I can see how badly you're hurt."

"It. . .it hurts somethin' fierce."

Stephen nodded. "I know. I'll be as careful as I can, but cleaning it will hurt some more. Can you stand it?"

"I guess I don't have a choice."

"What's your name?"

"Dan. Daniel Crews. From out Lexington way."

"Well, Dan Crews, if it gets to hurting too much, you just yell at me."

Liberty stuck his nose next to Dan's face and sniffed. Then he licked Dan's cheek and laid down beside him, resting his chin on Dan's shoulder. Dan reached out one shaking hand and rested it on Liberty's back. "That's my dog," Stephen said. "His leg was hurt awhile back."

"Did you fix it good?" Dan asked between clenched teeth as Stephen dabbed at his leg with a damp piece of Anna's apron.

"Yup. He limps a bit, but it doesn't stop him from going wherever he's a mind to."

Anna knelt beside Liberty and started telling Dan about the boys who'd attacked the dog. Stephen smiled at her. The tale would help keep Dan's mind off his pain.

The workman who'd fetched the bucket of water held Dan's ankle to keep his leg still while Stephen worked. Stephen was aware that most of the workmen in the area were standing about, watching. He didn't have time to wonder what they thought.

A minute later he heard horses' hooves thud against the ground behind him. "What's the problem?" an officer asked.

There was a babble as a number of men answered. It was Anna who finally explained. The officer knelt down and laid a hand on Dan's shoulder. "Keep courage, lad. Thank God there was a doctor's apprentice near."

Stephen glanced at the officer. "Lieutenant Andrews!" It was the kind officer he'd met at the common.

The lieutenant nodded sharply. "What can I do to help?"

"Is there a wagon we could use? I haven't any instruments with me or medicine. We can take him to Dr. Cuyler Allerton's."

Lieutenant Andrews gave sharp orders. Even while he continued to work, Stephen admired the way the man quickly arranged for a wagon pulled by two strong horses.

The lieutenant ordered hay put in the back of the wagon to make the ride easier for Dan. While the wagon was made ready, Stephen tied a clean piece of Anna's apron over the wounded leg with the apron's ties.

Watching Lieutenant Andrews and one of the workmen lift Dan into the wagon, Stephen frowned. He didn't like the look of that leg. It needed to be stitched up. He was afraid some of the nerves and muscles might have been cut by the bricks' sharp edges.

Half an hour later, Dan lay on the counter in the apothecary shop while Stephen watched Dr. Cuyler examine the leg.

"You're right," his uncle said, "we'll have to sew it up. One of the muscles is torn, but not badly."

Dr. Cuyler let Stephen sew up the badly wounded leg. The doctor held Dan's leg. Stephen bent over the leg, concentrating as he used the curved needle. He was sweating from trying so hard to do his work right. Every few minutes he rubbed his forehead against his shoulder so the sweat wouldn't run into his eyes.

He was almost through when the bells over the door tinkled cheerfully and Will entered. He came and stood beside Stephen, careful not to block the sunlight, but he didn't say anything.

Taking a deep breath, Stephen made the last stitch, tied a knot, and cut the thread.

The doctor smiled. "I couldn't have done better myself."

Dan groaned and opened his eyes. "Is it over?" Dr. Cuyler had given Dan laudanum to help him endure the pain, but like most patients, Dan had been awake through the stitching. Stephen saw Dan was sweating as much as he'd been. Dan squinted at Will. "What are you doin' here?"

"Heard about your accident and came to see how you are."

"I'm fine." He nodded toward Stephen. "Thanks to this lad." He looked from Stephen to Will and back again. "You two look a lot alike."

They both laughed. People had always said Stephen and Will looked alike. It was more true as Stephen grew older.

While Dr. Cuyler and Will talked with Dan, Stephen wiped his hands on a rag, then dipped water from a bucket into a basin and washed up.

Dr. Cuyler wanted Dan to stay in Boston for a couple days so he could keep a watch on Dan's leg. Patients usually stayed at home, but Dr. Cuyler sometimes let patients from out of town stay on a small bed in his library. He suggested Dan use it for a couple days.

"You won't be able to do hard labor at the Neck for a while. When the swelling goes down a bit, Stephen can use my carriage to take you back to your father's farm," Dr. Cuyler said.

Dr. Cuyler went home to ask Anna to bring a blanket and warm meal for Dan. Anna often had to help care for patients who stayed in the library.

After he'd left, Will grinned at Dan. "Took your patriotic duty a bit seriously, didn't you?"

Dan managed a small smile, though his lips were still pale from pain. "My load of bricks wasn't dumped on purpose. It was a true accident." Stephen thought he looked ashamed. "A British officer was barkin' at some workers, callin' them lazy, good-for-nothin's. I was laughin' inside and thinkin' if he only knew what we have in mind for the Neck, he'd be sayin' somethin' worse. Should have been watchin' where I was goin'."

Stephen frowned. "What are you two talking about?"

Will chuckled. "When General Gage needed people to help his soldiers build the wall, the Patriots made sure he got the kind of help *we* think he needs. The Patriots don't want the wall built. The Patriot workmen work slowly, do sloppy work, and tip over carts filled with supplies, but they make it all look like accidents. They even sunk a barge of bricks."

Stephen couldn't believe his ears. "I thought the bargeman ran into an unexpected reef and lost the bricks."

William grinned. "That's what we want people to think. We don't want Gage finding workers who might truly help him.

"Of course," Stephen muttered, wiping clean his needle.

Just then, Lieutenant Andrews stopped by to check on Dan's

leg. Stephen thought it was a nice thing for a busy officer to do. He wondered what Lieutenant Andrews would think if he knew why Dan had taken the job on the Neck!

Later Will and Stephen walked to the printing shop through the narrow streets, filled as always with redcoats. Paul Revere was waiting for them.

Will shook Paul's hand heartily. "Welcome back! Have you brought news of the Continental Congress?"

"That I have." He stepped past Will and Stephen, closed the heavy wooden door, and leaned against it. "There are serious things we must talk about."

"Yes." Will leaned back against the printing press and crossed his arms over his long brown vest. "General Gage didn't like the Suffolk Resolves you took to the Continental Congress. He believes they come too close to declaring war on Britain. On September first, he sent redcoats across the river. They took Charlestown's ammunition."

That had changed everything in Boston, Stephen thought. It had made everything worse between the redcoats and Patriots. People in all thirteen colonies were mad as hornets that the redcoats had stolen a town's arms. From the time the first English came to America, towns had always had to be ready to protect themselves. No one should take their guns and ammunition!

Will told Paul Revere about the Charlestown raid. Thousands of Massachusetts men had grabbed their guns and rushed from their villages and farms to help Charlestown. They were too late. The redcoats were already back in Boston.

General Gage was afraid the angry men would take the Neck road into Boston and attack the redcoats. His men had taken four cannons to the Neck to keep them out. Then his men had ruined Boston's cannons so they couldn't be used against the redcoats. He even sent a letter on a ship to England asking the king to send more redcoats to Boston.

It was because General Gage was afraid that he was building the wall on the Neck. "Gage started the wall to keep armed citizens out, but it will also keep redcoats and townspeople in Boston." Paul Revere turned his three-cornered hat in his hands. "People are upset about Charlestown, but maybe it's a blessing to the Patriots."

"How?" Will asked.

"It showed us that we need to warn the other towns when the troops are getting ready to leave Boston."

"How can we do that?" Stephen asked. "The redcoats won't tell Patriots the army's plans."

"That's why we need a group of watchers. Men to watch the army and see when they're getting ready to leave town, men to listen to everything redcoats say for a hint of their plans. Next time Gage plans a raid on a town's gunpowder, we want to get the news to the town first."

Stephen shifted uncomfortably. "Can we do that?"

"We must. We'll need a small band of trusted Patriots, about thirty men. Everyone will be sworn to secrecy."

Will nodded eagerly. "That's a good plan. We can call the group the Observers."

"We'll need a place to meet. What about this shop?"

"No." Will shook his head. "Redcoat officers are already suspicious about us. They'll be watching the shop."

Stephen cleared his throat. "Thirty men meeting in a home or shop would look suspicious, wouldn't they? What if they met at the Green Dragon Tavern? Will goes there all the time."

Paul Revere rubbed his thumb across his chin. "You're right. No one would think anything of men going to the tavern." He grinned at Stephen. "Are you ready to be a Son of Liberty?"

Stephen blinked in surprise. "I. . .I already help Will and Father print things for the Sons of Liberty."

"You can be a far greater help to us if you're willing."

Stephen gulped. "I wouldn't hurt anyone or their property. I want to be a doctor. I want to help people, not hurt them.

The silversmith nodded. "I respect you for that. You won't be asked to hurt anyone."

"Then, I'll be glad to help."

Paul Revere rested a hand on Stephen's shoulder. "As a doctor's apprentice, you have good reason to be about Boston. Dr. Allerton is a well-known Loyalist. British officers like and trust him. No one would suspect a boy in his shop of spying for the Patriots."

"S. . .spying?" Stephen wished his voice hadn't cracked. Mr. Revere was offering him an important job with the Patriots, and he sounded like a sick frog!

"If you don't want to, you needn't," Revere's calm voice reassured him.

Stephen sat up straight. He tried to ignore the painful way his heart was thumping away. He remembered the boys who'd helped with the tea party. Young Dan working for the Patriots on the Neck, right under the redcoats' noses. "I'll be a Patriot spy."

Will moved closer. "You'll need to keep your wits about you all the time. Never breathe a word about what you're asked to do to anyone but Paul and me."

"Will is right," Mr. Revere said. "With General Gage and

his army getting so jumpy, there's no telling what might happen if you're caught."

"I'll be careful." Stephen swallowed the lump that suddenly formed in his throat. "Tell me what you want me to do."

"Nothing right away, but be prepared. I've plans for you. Until then, keep your ears open around the redcoats. Pass along anything you see or hear to Will."

"Yes, sir." Stephen felt like he'd just stepped off a cliff and could never again get back to safety.

CHAPTER 7

The Warning

Stephen waited, frightened and excited, for his first orders as a spy. A month passed, and he still hadn't been asked to do anything scary for the Patriots. He hadn't heard the redcoats whisper any secrets, either.

Sitting in his parents' parlor, he glanced across the room at Anna. They used to share everything. The first secret he'd kept from her had been about the Boston Tea Party and Will's part in it ten months ago. Now he had another secret he couldn't share—he was a spy.

The room was filled with family tonight. Anna's family and Will's family were here. Shadows danced and darted over the families while they worked.

Stephen and Will sat close to the fireplace. They needed the light to repair the wool carders, pulling out broken wires and putting new ones in their place.

The soft whir of the great wheel as Stephen's mother spun the balls into yarn was a pleasant background to the family talk.

The family used to buy much of its yarn and material, but the harbor closing had changed all that. Most Patriots had agreed to make their own yarn and material, called home-spun, instead of buying it from Britain.

Stephen's sister, Lydia, and Anna were carding wool into soft balls. The wool cards were wooden paddles with hundreds of short wire teeth. The wool was placed between two cards and combed to remove dirt and tangles. The cards' teeth made a scratching sound, like Liberty's claws when he pawed at a door to get out.

"It's so nice to spend an evening with family instead of strangers!" Anna said, pulling a fluff of wool from between her cards.

"I think it was wonderful of you to take that family into your home," Eliza said, looking up from her mending.

"Yes," Kathleen agreed. She was making a pair of breeches for Stephen, which he badly needed! "But it must be difficult having strangers living with you."

"It certainly is!" Anna said.

"Remember, Anna, it could have been our family chased from our home," her mother reminded her. Aunt Abigail sat at the small clock wheel, winding the yarn from the great wheel onto small wooden reels.

No one said anything for a minute. Everyone knew Aunt Abigail meant if the Patriots were chasing Loyalists from their homes in other towns, it could happen in Boston, too. And everyone in the room except Aunt Abigail and Anna were Patriots.

"The Patriots are wrong to chase people from their homes," Stephen's mother said quietly. "We can all agree on that."

Everyone nodded.

Raised voices came from the hallway.

"It sounds like our fathers are arguing again," Anna said.

Stephen recognized the pain and fright he saw in her eyes. It was the same pain and fright he felt when their fathers fought. He wasn't sure why it frightened him, but it did.

He took a deep breath. It had been such a pleasant evening, with everyone working together and visiting. Now the day would end unhappily.

His father and Dr. Cuyler entered the parlor, still arguing. They stopped nose to nose and toe to toe. Dr. Cuyler waved a copy of the *Boston Observer* in one hand. "How can you print such things?"

Father crossed his arms. "We only printed what the Continental Congress in Philadelphia said."

Dr. Cuyler's eyes sparked. "You printed that Americans should not buy anything from Britain until Parliament gives up the tea tax, reopens Boston Harbor, and lets Massachusetts be run by its old charter."

"It's a peaceful way to try to get Parliament to change its mind," Father observed. "What's wrong with that?"

Dr. Cuyler shook the paper right in his brother-in-law's face. "It's what you printed next that's wrong! The congress said if the redcoats attack people here, the other colonies will send troops to help Boston."

Father grabbed the paper, crumpling it with one hand. "You think that is wrong?"

"They've almost declared war on Britain, on our own government!" Dr. Cuyler pushed his wig back from his forehead.

Stephen would have laughed at how funny Dr. Cuyler looked with his wig sliding off the back of his head, but he was feeling too sick to his stomach at the word "war." Everyone seemed to be using that word these days.

"John Hancock is the leader of the congress," Stephen's father said. "He says we should ask God to forgive the sins that have caused our trouble with Old England. And to ask God's help in becoming friendly with England again."

Anna took a deep breath. "That sounds like the Patriots want peace, not war, Father."

Dr. Cuyler snorted. "Don't be fooled, Anna. The congress also said it's a Christian's duty to fight bad leaders. But the Bible says we are to obey our leaders."

"The Bible also says that rulers must be just and rule in the fear of God," Father argued. "God wants kings to treat people well so they can live in peace and have good lives."

Will stepped in. "Until King George III rules the way the Bible says he should, we will serve no king but King Jesus."

That was the Patriots' slogan, Stephen remembered. The words always sent a shiver of awe and pride through him. It seemed a great thing to choose to serve Jesus. But he knew the words only angered Loyalists like Dr. Cuyler and his family.

Dr. Cuyler's fists bunched at his sides. "The congress called the king a tyrant."

Father's face grew red. "When a king uses his power to hurt people instead of help them, he *is* a tyrant."

"Bah!" Dr. Cuyler waved both hands at him. "You make your living with words. You can make anything sound true. It's treason to declare war against the king. Treason! Until you admit as much, we're no longer friends!"

"That's fine with me!" Father roared.

Dr. Cuyler grabbed Anna's hand. "Come Anna, Abigail. We're leaving."

Stephen stared openmouthed as Dr. Cuyler hurried toward the door. Anna tried to keep up with him, staring back over her shoulder, tripping over her skirt and petticoat. Her blue eyes were wide as her gaze met Stephen's. Aunt Abigail followed after them, shaking her head.

Stephen's stomach clenched. What he and Anna had feared had happened—their fathers' arguments had broken their friendship.

The women quietly put their work away and went into the kitchen. Even Lydia was too shocked to try saying anything. Will poked at the cold fireplace. Father picked up the wrinkled newspaper and pretended to read it. Did they think that by not talking about what had happened, it would just go away?

The three of them jumped at a pounding on the front door. Stephen grabbed the candlestick and hurried to answer. When he opened the door, the breeze blew the flame sideways, but it didn't go out.

There was no one on the door stoop. Only a house away, he saw two redcoats walking swiftly. One looked back over his shoulder with a wicked grin. Lieutenant Rand!

Why had he pounded on the door if he didn't want to come inside? A flutter caught Stephen's eye. A handbill nailed to the door! Stephen yanked it off and carried it back to the parlor.

"Who was it?" his father asked.

Stephen mumbled an answer. At the top of the paper was a skull and crossbones. It made his skin crawl.

He set the candlestick and paper on a small, round pie-crust table beside a wing chair. He didn't want his father and brother to see how badly his hands were shaking.

"What is that?" his father asked, coming to stand beside him. A moment later, Will joined them.

Stephen explained, then read it aloud. When he got to the end, his voice was shaking as badly as his hands. "If fighting breaks out between the Patriots and the British troops, the Patriots' leaders will be destroyed."

Father grunted. "Destroyed is a nice way to say they'll be tried in England and hung as traitors."

The paper listed Sam Adams, John Hancock, and a few others.

"Is that all it says?" Will leaned over his younger brother's shoulder.

Stephen read the rest. "Those trumpeters of evil, the printers, will not be forgotten." A list of Patriot printers followed. His father's and Will's names were at the top of the list.

CHAPTER 8
A Secret Code

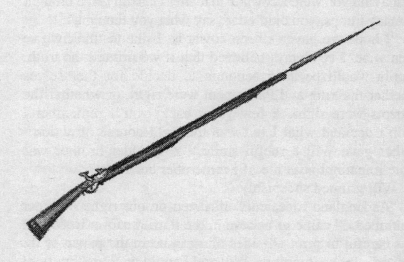

Destroyed! Hung! Threats against his very own father and brother! Fear swept through Stephen like a wildfire. The skull and crossbones seemed to laugh at him in the candlelight.

His father picked up the paper, holding it so the candle's

light fell on it. "So, William, it's come."

"Yes."

Stephen stared at them. How could they sound so calm? Hadn't they heard what the paper said? "Father, they've threatened your life and William's."

His father, still bent over the paper, glanced at him from beneath thick black-and-gray eyebrows. "Before we can be hung, we must be brought to trial and found guilty of treason against Britain and the king. We have only printed what the congress and others said. We haven't said we agreed with them."

"That's why you've been so careful," Stephen said slowly. "Anna said you were a coward, that after General Gage brought so many troops, you didn't dare say what you thought."

"I hope we haven't been cowards. I like to think we've been wise. I've always believed that if we printed the truth, people would be smart enough to decide for themselves whether the king and Parliament were right, or whether the Patriots were right. A few years back, you'll remember I hadn't decided what I felt was the right course of action." Father gave Will a rueful smile. "Your older brother was quite impatient with me, if I remember correctly."

Will grinned sheepishly.

"As England repeatedly infringed on our rights," Father continued, "I came to believe in the Patriot cause. But I still was careful to print all sides of an issue in the paper. If we printed our own opinions, Will and I could be found guilty of treason. It might come to that yet, but I hope not."

Stephen felt sweaty all over. "Will you be arrested?"

"We can only wait and see."

William patted his shoulder. "I'm sure whoever wrote this is only trying to frighten us."

His father nodded. "General Gage has tried to buy us, to pay us to print only things the British government liked. Lieutenant Rand threatened us the other day. Now this."

Stephen sat up a little straighter. "I think Lieutenant Rand nailed this to our door. I saw him on the street."

His father sighed. "It would be like him to use his position to try to bully us. Thank God all the British officers aren't like him." He folded the paper in half. "I'd best let your mother know about this before she hears it from someone else." He walked slowly to the kitchen, where the women were spinning and carding wool beside the huge fireplace.

Will took down the old musket that hung over the fireplace. He ran a hand along the barrel. The musket had been there for as long as Stephen could remember. "Do you think it works?" Stephen asked.

"I don't know. I'm not sure we can get ammunition for it. It's awfully old. Our great-grandfather, Robert, carried it to war against the French in 1710. He fought alongside the British soldiers then. Now if we fight with it, we'll be fighting against the British."

Stephen's throat tightened. "Robert was killed in that war. Our grandfather, his only child, was born while he was fighting, remember? He never even saw his son."

William nodded.

Stephen swallowed hard and stuck his hands in his breeches' deep pockets. "Do you think that might happen to your son Paul if you fight? If you were. . .if you were killed—" Stephen gulped. He hadn't thought it would be so hard to say that. "You'd never see Paul again. He's only two. He might not even remember you when he grows up."

"I know." Will's words were so low that Stephen almost

didn't hear them. Will carefully hung the musket back in place. "I've joined the minutemen."

"I thought you would."

"I talked it over with Eliza first," Will said. "I do think about Paul. I worry what will happen to him and Eliza if we go to war. But Eliza and I agreed that when Paul grows up, we want him to have the rights Englishmen have had for more than five hundred years—even if that means I have to fight."

Stephen didn't know what to say.

"What about you?"

Stephen frowned. "What do you mean?"

"If war comes, will you fight with the Patriots?"

Stephen shrugged and kicked at a bit of ash on the floor with the toe of his shoe. "I won't fight against them."

Will grinned. "I didn't think you would, but that's no answer. You're fourteen, almost a man."

Stephen squared his shoulders. "I don't know if I can try to kill anyone. I want to be a doctor and save lives. Have you ever seen anyone die?"

William shook his head. "No."

"I have, lots of times. It's terrible. I know that if they love Jesus' people go to heaven when they die. It's still hard when Dr. Cuyler and I try everything we know to keep them alive and nothing works." He pressed his lips together hard and spread his hands. "Do you understand? When I know how hard it is to save a life, how can I choose to kill? It's much easier to take a life than save one."

Would Will understand? He must! He loved Will. He was proud that his older brother was a Son of Liberty and an Observer and a minuteman. He wanted Will to be just as proud of him.

"You have a good head on your shoulders, Stephen. You don't let anyone push you into anything you don't believe in. That's good. But what if everyone refused to fight and let King George take away all our rights? What would our children and grandchildren say when they found out we'd let rights Englishmen have had for more than five hundred years be taken away without a fight? If war comes, you may not have a choice but to fight. The only choice left will be which side you fight for."

Stephen's gaze slid to the musket, almost hidden now in the room's dark shadows. A coldness as strong as the metal on the musket's barrel wrapped itself tightly around his chest.

The next morning, Stephen stood outside the apothecary door, beneath the creaking sign with the mortar and pestle. His hands were bunched into fists at his sides. Did he dare go inside? Dr. Cuyler was so angry with his father. What if he didn't want Stephen for an apprentice anymore? Maybe Dr. Cuyler wouldn't even want him and Anna to be friends!

Well, he wouldn't find out standing on the street. Stephen took a deep breath, pretending he was breathing in courage, and went inside.

Dr. Cuyler looked up from his account book. "Stephen, I'm glad you're here! I was afraid your father might not let you come after last night."

The weight of the world seemed to drop from Stephen's chest. "He didn't tell me I couldn't come, but I was afraid you might not want me."

Dr. Cuyler laid down his quill. His gaze met Stephen's. "My argument is with your father, not with you. I count you not only my apprentice and nephew, but my friend."

"Thank you, sir, but I. . .I'm a Patriot, too, like Father."

"Do you think King George is a tyrant?"

"I'm not sure. When I hear you talk about what you believe about the king and our rights, what you say sounds right. But I think what Father believes is more right, and I believe what Father believes."

"At least you listen to both sides. You aren't encouraging anyone to fight like your father is."

"No, sir." Stephen frowned. He wished Dr. Cuyler respected his father more.

"Your father is a stubborn man." Dr. Cuyler grinned. "But your aunt Abigail says I'm one, too. Don't worry yourself over your father and me. We've been angry at each other before. We'll work things out eventually. Now, let's get to work. There are some plants in the medical garden that need to be picked and dried."

In spite of Dr. Cuyler's assurances, Stephen wasn't convinced the men would work things out. The two had quarreled a lot through the years, but Stephen had never seen them as angry at each other as they were now. At least Dr. Cuyler still wanted him to be his apprentice. He was glad this one thing in his life was the same.

At eleven o'clock, Anna came by with lunch for her father and Dan.

"I knew you'd bring your own lunch," she said to Stephen, "but I brought you a piece of apple pie."

"Great!"

She wrinkled her nose. "Not too great. It's Boston Tea Party apple pie. We're out of sugar and good flour, so I sweetened it with honey, and the crust is of cornmeal."

"I'm sure it will be good." All the women in town were

using substitutes in their cooking. With the port closed, many of the foods they were used to using couldn't be found in Boston or were too expensive to buy.

"Mother and I try to make a game of it, figuring out how to make our favorite dishes using different foods. Some things turn out better than others."

Stephen thought Anna was being a good sport about it. After all, it wasn't the Loyalists' fault the port was closed, but they suffered just like the Patriots.

"I saw a handbill this morning," Anna said slowly. "It had a skull and crossbones at the top. Have you seen it?"

Stephen nodded. The memory of that handbill made his throat dry.

"I couldn't believe your father and Will were threatened that way. I think it's awful!"

"Father says nothing can happen to them without a trial, and they haven't done anything wrong."

"Still, I'm a bit afraid for them, aren't you?"

Stephen nodded. "Yes, I am."

He tried to ignore the fear that coiled in his stomach as he went back to work.

Two days later, the musket was gone from over the fireplace. Stephen didn't ask where it went. He didn't hear anyone else in the family ask, either. Likely they thought the same thing he did: that Will had found a way to sneak the musket into hiding, probably even out of Boston. Patriots were collecting weapons in case of war.

Then something more exciting pushed all thought of the musket from his mind. He was given a spy assignment! Dr. Cuyler had asked Stephen to take Dan home to his farm near

Lexington. When Will and Paul Revere heard, they told him it was very important to get some copies of the *Boston Observer* to Buckman's Tavern in Lexington.

"There's a hidden message in the newspaper," William had said, stacking the single sheets into a pile.

Stephen had laughed. "You can't hide anything in a newspaper!"

"The best place to hide anything is right in plain sight." Will's eyes twinkled with fun. "The message becomes clear when the reader uses a mask to read it."

"You're funning me. How can wearing a mask help? Maybe the mask has spectacles with magic glass," he teased back.

"It's not that kind of mask. The reader doesn't wear the mask. He lays the mask over the newspaper. Like this."

Will showed Stephen a cutout of the picture that was always printed at the top of the *Boston Observer*. It was a man looking through a telescope. The inside of the picture had been cut out.

Will laid the mask over the covered page. "See for yourself."

Stephen grinned. "You're just waiting for me to make a fool of myself and try to find a secret message where there is none. Like the time I was six and you told me there were fish in Mill Pond that could walk. I fished and watched for those walking fish for weeks before Kathleen told me you were only teasing!"

Will crossed his arms over his vest and chuckled. "This is no walking fish, I promise. Look."

Stephen looked. The mask was small. The opening only covered ten lines of the tiny type, and two of the six narrow columns. The message inside the cutout included words from more than one column. Stephen's mouth dropped open as he read them. "Why, this says—"

Will clapped a hand that smelled strongly of ink and leather over Stephen's mouth. "Never repeat a message aloud, even when you think you're alone or with someone you can trust, like now. You only need to be wrong one time to get in a lot of trouble."

Stephen nodded slowly.

Will took away his hand. "Now that redcoats are checking everyone who comes into and leaves Boston, the Patriots are trying new ways to get messages to each other safely. Sometimes the messages will be true. Sometimes they will be false, used only to test whether people can be trusted or are spies for the British. You're never to tell *anyone* you're carrying a message or what it says."

"I won't. I give my word."

Will grinned. "Your word is always good enough for me."

Stephen felt embarrassed but proud. "How does the person who gets the message know what part of the paper to put the mask over so he reads the right words?"

"That's a secret you'll never know."

CHAPTER 9
Escape from Boston

Dan and Liberty sat beside Stephen in Dr. Cuyler's carriage. Every once in a while Dan's leg bounced against the side when a wooden wheel rolled over a rock or rut. Dan would grunt and dig his teeth into his bottom lip, but he never complained. Stephen admired him for that. He knew Dan's leg was still mighty sore and would be for weeks.

"Whoa." Stephen pulled on the reins, bringing Dr. Cuyler's small bay mare to a stop at the town gate on the Neck. Redcoats were checking everyone who left town now. In front of them a farmer with an empty cart waited patiently behind another farmer with an empty wagon.

One of the redcoats knelt down and looked beneath the wagon, then stood and felt beneath the hard wooden seat the farmer sat upon. A moment later he waved the farmer on.

"They're lookin' for guns," Dan said in a low voice. "They've heard Patriots are sneakin' guns out of Boston."

Goose bumps ran up and down Stephen's arms. Had Will slipped the musket past the guards somehow?

"Yelp!" Liberty's bark startled Stephen. In a flash, the skinny dog scrambled across his lap and leaped from the carriage after a squirrel.

"Liberty, stop!"

Liberty ignored him. The squirrel darted under the farmer's moving wagon. Liberty headed after him. Stephen leaped up. Liberty was going to be run over! "Stop, Liberty!"

A farmer with a cart in front of them dove for Liberty. He caught his skinny tail and held tight. Liberty yelped a complaint. The farmer yanked him back, saving him from the wagon's rumbling wheels.

He handed Liberty up to Stephen with a friendly grin.

"Thank you, sir. Guess you saved his life."

"A life worth saving, I'm sure. Have a dog of me own I wouldn't trade for King George's palace."

The soldiers were searching the farmer's cart. It didn't take long. When they waved the farmer on, he gave them a jaunty salute before starting.

"Halt!" One of the soldiers pointed his musket at the farmer. "I know you! Deserter!"

Stephen's heart seemed to leap to his throat. He watched, stunned, as the soldiers arrested the man who'd cheerfully saved Liberty's life.

Stephen and Dan looked at each other. A deserter! Dan shrugged nervously. "We've nothin' to worry 'bout. We're not sneakin' anyone or anything out of town."

Stephen's foot touched the pile of newspapers on the floor. Dan didn't know they carried a Patriot secret.

The redcoat checking the cart waved the farmer on. Stephen urged the horse forward. The soldier looked underneath the carriage. Then he ordered Stephen and Dan out.

Stephen forced himself to not look at the newspapers. He wrapped the reins around the brake handle and climbed down. "Dan has a bad leg," he told the soldier. "He hurt it working on the wall here on the Neck. Can he stay in the carriage? It still hurts him a lot to walk on it."

The soldier looked into the carriage and reached for Dan's leg. His hand stopped above the bandages. Dan had no stocking on that leg. It was still too swollen and too heavily wrapped for a stocking to fit. "Stay where you are, then," he told Dan.

The soldier pointed to the pile. "Are those rebel Patriot newspapers or Loyalist newspapers?"

"Just newspapers, sir." *Pretend everything is normal,* he reminded himself. "The editor prints facts, not opinions."

The redcoat grunted. "I'll be deciding that for myself. Let me see one of them rags."

Dan untied the twine that held the papers together and handed him one off the top.

The soldier glanced over it. "Why, this tells all about that rebel Patriot congress in Philadelphia!" His eyes looked like small black beads as he glared over the top of the page at Stephen. "Says the colonies should train their armies in case we attack them! What do you mean saying this isn't a rebel paper?"

"Only tells what the congress said, sir. Doesn't tell the readers to do as the congress asks. Besides, there's a Loyalist handbill we're carrying as well."

Stephen pulled out a handbill topped by a skull and crossbones and handed it to the soldier. It was the same handbill that threatened his father's and Will's lives. "You see, the editor prints news for both Patriots and Loyalists."

"You the printer's apprentice?" The soldier raised one black eyebrow and eyed Stephen suspiciously.

"Oh, no, sir! I'm Dr. Allerton's apprentice. This is his carriage. I'm taking his patient home to his farm."

The soldier grunted again. "Dr. Allerton's a good Loyalist."

"Yes, sir. Can't find a man more loyal to the king."

"Sure wish I hadn't hurt this leg." Dan rubbed his knee and shook his head. "Wanted to keep helpin' build that wall for General Gage. Lot more excitin' than farmin'."

The redcoat handed Dan back the paper and handbill. "Have any good fishing streams on that farm?"

"The best in Massachusetts, sir. I plan to take Stephen fishin' there today."

"Maybe you'll bring a few back for me?" The soldier grinned, showing three of his teeth were missing on one side of his mouth.

"Be glad to, sir." Stephen climbed back into the carriage.

He and Dan waved and smiled at the soldier as they drove off. When they'd gone about one hundred feet, Stephen let his breath out in a whoosh. "I didn't think he was going to let us take those papers with us."

"Me, either. Redcoats have good guns and cannons, but it's words that scare them."

They both laughed at that.

Stephen hadn't been out of Boston in months. He felt free out on the road.

Dan rode with Stephen into Lexington to deliver the papers. It was easy to find Buckman's Tavern, a two-story wooden building with two chimneys. It stood by the town common, called Lexington Green. The road ran right past the green.

The tavern master gave no hint that he knew the papers held a secret message. Stephen wondered if he was the man the message was for. Maybe it was one of the tavern workers or a stable boy who watched the guests' horses. Could it be the craftsman who walked in and bought a copy almost right away?

A spy could be anyone, Stephen realized. He chuckled. Who, for instance, would think *he* was a spy?

"What's so funny?" Dan asked.

"Just glad to be out of Boston for a change." Stephen couldn't stop grinning. Knowing he'd done well on his spy mission—getting the papers out of Boston without any redcoats finding the secret message—made him feel ten feet tall.

The tavern keeper gave the boys each a mug of cold apple cider. They took their drinks outside and sat on the edge of the green beneath a large oak tree. The ground was covered with brown, musty-smelling leaves. They crackled and poked through Stephen's knee-length socks. The dampness from the earth seeped through the leaves and through the bottom of

Stephen's breeches, but he hardly noticed.

The Lexington minutemen were practicing on the green. The boys watched. Stephen wished Boston's minutemen had a good place to practice in Boston. They couldn't practice on Boston Common with the redcoats living and training there.

Watching the men, Stephen's heart sank as fast as a rock to the bottom of one of Boston's ponds. Lexington's army looked like a ragtag group of boys playing at war compared to the redcoats. The minutemen were dressed in their everyday work clothes: craftsmen in leather breeches and rough shirts, farmers in frocks, storekeepers and town leaders in fancy greatcoats and long vests. No one wore a uniform.

Not one carried a musket as fine as the redcoats' muskets. Instead they held squirrel and duck rifles or old muskets like the one that had hung over the Lankford fireplace. A few men who'd fought in the French and Indian Wars years ago had swords at their sides. No one had a bayonet like the redcoats had on the ends of their muskets.

The minutemen didn't snap to orders with sharp attention like the redcoats on Boston Common. They didn't move as one person to the officers' orders.

Stephen wondered whether they even knew how poorly they compared to the redcoats. The men tramping through the crisp leaves beneath the bright blue sky were eagerly trying to follow commands, their eyes shining, their faces excited.

"Why don't they practice shooting?" he asked Dan.

"Savin' their bullets. With General Gage and his men raidin' towns' ammunition, we don't dare waste any."

The longer Stephen and Dan watched, the sadder Stephen grew. Will was part of Boston's minutemen. Were they as poorly furnished and trained as these men? If a war started, what chance did Will and the minutemen have against the redcoats?

"I'm goin' to join the minutemen," Dan said, "soon's my leg's better."

"Do you have a gun?"

"Only an old squirrel gun, but I can shoot with it." Dan leaned back against the tree. "Shot lots of squirrels and rabbits and such. A man should be easy to hit."

Stephen's stomach turned over at the thought of shooting a man like he was wild game.

When the practice was over, a boy carrying a large drum and a handful of men with fifes started playing "Yankee Doodle" and started across the green. The minutemen fell in behind them. They headed toward a large wooden building beside Buckman's Tavern.

Stephen jumped up. "Where are they going?"

"To the meeting house. A Patriot minister will give them a sermon tellin' them to fight bravely for God and their country."

Dan kept his word and took Stephen fishing at a stream that ran through his father's property. It was the most fun Stephen had had in a long time. When later that afternoon Stephen headed back to Boston, a huge basket with sixty smelly perch sat on the floor beside him.

Dan's father and mother sent back pumpkins, corn, and flour for the doctor. "There's barely room left for me," Stephen had told Dan with a grin.

Stephen didn't forget the soldier at the gate. When he arrived there late that evening, he gave him a dozen fish. The soldier grinned from ear to ear as he piled them on the ground beside the gate, where they would lie until the soldier was off duty.

"Remember that deserter we caught this afternoon?" the soldier asked, taking the last fish Stephen handed him.

Stephen's heart thumped so hard he could barely hear himself think. Why would the redcoat ask him about the deserter? Had he somehow learned Stephen had slipped a secret message out of town beneath his nose in the *Boston Observer?*

He gulped and wiped his hand on his breeches. "Sure, I remember. He was dressed like a farmer."

"They shot him this afternoon on the common." The soldier grinned. "General Gage came out personally to tell me and the other guard here how well we'd done in capturing him."

"Congratulations," Stephen said in a shaky voice. "Good night, sir. Enjoy your fish." He reached for the reins and slapped them lightly against the horse's rump.

Other redcoat deserters had been shot, but Stephen hadn't known who they were. He hadn't seen them captured only a few feet from freedom. They hadn't smiled at him and saved his dog.

He was going to be sick.

CHAPTER 10

A Dangerous Mission

Six weeks later, Stephen gritted his teeth when he entered his home after working at Dr. Cuyler's all day. The first thing he heard was the voice he'd grown to dislike so much: Lieutenant Rand's. He wondered for the hundredth time how Lieutenant Rand had been assigned to live in their house!

It was November, and winter was coming. Many British

officers were staying in townspeople's houses. Quartering, it was called.

Stephen stepped softly past the parlor, where the officers were visiting, toward the stairs leading to the second floor. Firelight and candlelight gave a mellow glow to the parlor. The hallway was dark, as it was already past candlelighting time.

Until the officers had moved in, the family had saved scarce wood and candles by keeping the parlor closed. They visited by the kitchen fireplace instead. There the wood could be used for three things at once: It heated the room, heated food, and heated water for washing and chores.

"You there, boy!" Lieutenant Rand's voice stopped him.

Stephen sighed and walked into the warm parlor. The officer must have heard the door open and been watching for him. "Yes, sir?"

"See that you polish my boots tonight."

Stephen's cheeks grew hot. He pressed his lips hard together to keep from telling the officer to polish his own boots. His father had warned all the family to treat the officers like guests. "Yes, Lieutenant Rand."

"See you do a better job than you did last week."

"Yes, sir." Stephen looked at the other officer, who stood before the fireplace with his elbow on the mantle, frowning at Lieutenant Rand. "Shall I polish your boots, too, Lieutenant Andrews?"

The senior officer smiled at him. "No, but it was kind of you to offer."

Stephen nodded at both men and made his way upstairs. At least Lieutenant Andrews acted kindly toward the family. Still, he didn't like having the officers in his home.

The officers had taken over the bedchamber William shared with his wife, Eliza, and their son, Paul. Now William's family used Stephen's bedchamber. Stephen slept on the high-backed wooden settle beside the kitchen fireplace.

He tried not to complain about it. Officers were quartered all over town. Dr. Cuyler and Uncle Ethan both had officers staying with them. Anna was grumpier than ever, sharing her home with both the officers and the Loyalist family. She blamed the Patriots for causing the soldiers to be in Boston.

He slipped into his parents' room and laid down on their featherbed. Just thinking about the hard settle made this bed feel wonderful!

"Are you ill?"

Stephen jumped at Will's voice. His brother stood in the doorway, holding a brass candleholder. The small flame waved, sending shadows over Will's face.

"No," Stephen answered. "I just wanted to get away from the officers, even if it is cold up here."

William's easy grin spread across his face. "I don't blame you." He set the candle on the stand beside the door and sat down on the foot of the bed. The mattress sank under his weight. "I need to talk with you," Will whispered. "After dinner, I'll make some excuse for the two of us to go to the print shop."

Stephen slipped his hands behind his head and frowned. "Why not talk here?"

"Walls have ears these days."

Stephen nodded. With the officers here, it wasn't safe for the family to talk about Patriot matters in their own home. He wondered what could be so important that they had to go somewhere tonight to talk. Could the Sons of Liberty have another spying assignment for him?

A little later when he went downstairs to join the family for dinner, Kathleen and Lieutenant Andrews were in the doorway between the parlor and hallway. He wondered why Kathleen was smiling up at the British officer in that funny, sugary sweet way with her cheeks all pink. Could Kathleen *like* Lieutenant Andrews? Not just friendly-like, but as a woman likes a man? Could Kathleen like someone that way who wasn't a Patriot?

When they finished dinner, Lieutenant Rand pushed back his chair. "I'll have a cup of tea in the parlor, Miss Kathleen. See that it's good English tea—none of your rebel Patriot brew."

Everyone stopped talking and stared at him. Finally Kathleen stood. Her long red curls reflected the light from the few candles that burned on the table. "I'll be glad to bring you tea, sir," her voice trembled, "but I'm afraid it will be raspberry leaf tea. We don't serve English tea in this house. English tea has brought too much trouble to our town."

Lieutenant Rand threw down his napkin. "No lady in England would treat a guest like this!"

"Lieutenant Rand!" Lieutenant Andrews sounded shocked.

Father leaped up. "Apologize to my daughter!"

Lieutenant Rand snorted and ignored Father's demand.

Kathleen paid no attention. "Lieutenant Rand, in Boston, no gentleman asks for anything he knows his host is not able or willing to give."

Good for her! Stephen thought, pounding his fist against his knee beneath the table.

Red color started at Lieutenant Rand's neck and rushed up over his face to his wig. He turned to Lieutenant Andrews. "If anyone asks for me this evening, I'll be at Dr. Allerton's." He glared over his shoulder at Kathleen. "The Allertons know how to treat their guests." He stomped toward the door, his boots thunking against the floor.

Will gave Stephen a strange look. "I didn't know Lieutenant Rand knew Dr. Cuyler."

Stephen nodded. "Officers are quartered there, too. They use Dr. Cuyler's library in the evenings instead of going to the taverns like most soldiers. Anna doesn't like it much. They expect us to wait on them."

"I apologize for our officers," Lieutenant Andrews said. "I know it's hard for people to have us living in their homes. Please remember that it's hard for the officers, too. They'd rather be in their own homes with their own families back in England."

Kathleen smiled at him. "Of course they would."

Stephen wondered again how Kathleen felt about the kind, good-looking young officer.

A few minutes later, Stephen and Will were headed toward the print shop, their cloaks wrapped tightly against the cold November wind whipping through Boston's narrow streets. They had to watch where they were going, as the streetlights weren't lit. The town had only had streetlights for a year and a half. Stephen had thought they were the most wonderful invention he'd ever seen. He liked watching the men climb their ladders each night with their oil cans to light the lamps. Now the town couldn't even use them. The town wasn't buying oil for them when money was so tight.

Stephen wondered all the way to the printing shop what Will would tell him. The redcoats they passed in the street reminded him why they had to be so cautious. A fourth of the people in Boston now were British soldiers. Many of the other people were Loyalists. Patriots had to be careful what they said everywhere.

"Brrr! It's almost as cold inside as out!" Stephen rubbed his mittened hands together after entering the shop.

Will reached in his pocket for a flint to light a candle. The flint sparked. A candlewick flared. Its yellow flame gave a small circle of light but left most of the room with its press and piles of paper in dark shadows.

"What do you have to tell me?" Stephen couldn't wait any longer!

Will hiked himself onto the wooden worktable beside the candle. "The Observers have another assignment for you."

Stephen's heartbeat quickened, but he tried to sound calm. "Do they want me to sneak more newspapers out of town?"

"No. This is far more dangerous."

"What. . .what is it?"

"A redcoat wants to desert. He needs help getting out of Boston."

Stephen shivered. He remembered the deserter arrested at the Neck. "Deserters are killed if they're caught."

"Yes."

"What happens to people who help them?"

"Prison. Still want to help us?"

Stephen took a deep breath. This was scarier than he'd thought it would be. "Yes, but I don't see how I can get anyone past the guards on the Neck in Dr. Cuyler's carriage."

"You won't need to. You just need to hide him for one night, give him different clothes to wear, and hide his uniform."

"Where can *I* hide him? Officers are living with us! Do you mean to hide him here in the print shop?"

"No. The redcoats are watching this place too closely. We

want you to hide him at Dr. Cuyler's for a few hours."

Stephen frowned. "The apothecary is full of officers and Loyalists. How could I hide him there? Oh! It's like the hidden message in the newspaper, isn't it? The best place to hide something or someone is in plain sight."

"Something like that. No one will think it strange to see a soldier go into a Loyalist doctor's place. Now, here's the plan."

CHAPTER 11

The Deserter

Stephen was so excited he didn't fall asleep until very late. He tossed and turned on the hard settle, trying to think where he could hide the deserter at Dr. Cuyler's.

When he finally did fall asleep, he dreamed both he and the deserter were standing in front of a redcoats' firing squad!

He woke up sweating.

Kathleen was already stirring the ashes in the kitchen fireplace, fanning the warm embers from the night before into flame. "Good morning, sleepyhead," she said. "I've already filled the water kettle. When the water's warm, you can take a pitcher to the officers. Lieutenant Rand bellows if he doesn't have it as soon as he awakes."

Stephen stretched and yawned. "Nothing pleases him."

"My waffles please both the officers." Kathleen set the two-handled waffle iron over the fire to heat. "We won't have them again for a while. We haven't much good flour left."

Stephen pulled a wooden comb through his hair and tied it in back with a thin strip of leather. "Last week I polished Lieutenant Rand's boots until I could see myself in them, and—"

"I saw his boots in the hall outside his door this morning."

Stephen leaped up. The stone floor was cold on his bare feet. "Yipes! I forgot to polish his boots last night!" He was off in a flash. Maybe he could polish them before the grumpy officer awoke.

He breathed a sigh of relief when the boots were polished and set back outside the officers' door. Lieutenant Rand didn't even thank him, but Stephen didn't mind. At least the officer hadn't complained he'd done a poor job again.

Kathleen's crisp waffles did please the officer, just as she'd said, and the lieutenants went off to their duties in good moods.

While Kathleen and Lydia cleaned up the breakfast dishes, Mother helped Stephen gather clothes for the deserter. In her bedchamber, they folded the clothes and put them in a burlap sack.

"That's everything Will told me he wanted," she said, tucking in the last item.

Will had told Stephen not to tell anyone about the deserter, but they'd had to tell their mother so they could get the clothes they needed.

Stephen could see the worry in her eyes when she handed him the bag. "I wish Will hadn't dragged you into this," she said.

"We have to help the deserter, don't we?"

"Yes, but you're so young, and this is so dangerous."

She'd never stop thinking of him as a baby! "Father and Will would do what's right, even if it were dangerous. So would you."

She sighed and touched his cheek. "I'm proud you agreed to help this man, but I'm frightened for you, too. Don't forget anything Will told you, and don't tell anyone else about this man and what you're doing."

"I won't." He knew if she wasn't such a strong Patriot, she'd never let him do this. She'd stormed at Will when he'd told her about the plan.

At the door, Stephen turned and looked back at her. "I'll be careful, Mother. I promise."

She smiled, but he could still see the worry in her green eyes.

That day at the apothecary, the plan was all Stephen could think about. He didn't know when the deserter would show up. The deserter would have to watch closely for a chance to get away from the other redcoats without raising suspicion.

Stephen watched for the deserter all day. And all the next day. The third day, he wondered if the soldier would ever show up. He forgot about him for hours at a time while he worked.

It was long past candle-lighting time when Stephen finally began closing up the shop. Before he finished, the officers quartered with Dr. Cuyler's family came in. Stephen carried wood and started a fire for them in the library fireplace while one of the officers lit what seemed a wasteful number of candles.

His hand was on the door latch when he heard the knock on the door. A redcoat with brown curly hair stood there. He wasn't an officer. "Are you looking for the officers, sir?"

"No, I'm looking for a doctor. I've cut my hand."

"The doctor's visiting patients. I'm his apprentice. Come in." Stephen placed a tin lantern on a table. He unwrapped the bloody cloth and studied the wound in the light.

"I was polishing my bayonet," the redcoat said, "and it slipped. How bad is the cut?"

"Not as bad as it looks," Stephen said. "Even though it bled a lot, it will be fine when the wound heals."

The man gave a large sigh of relief. "Good." He set his hat on the table. "What's your name?"

"Stephen Lankford." He started to stand. The soldier's good hand clamped Stephen's shoulder and stopped him. Stephen's head jerked up in surprise.

"God bless the Liberty Boys," the man whispered.

Stephen blinked. That was the code Will had said the deserter would use!

The library door swung open and Captain Ingles came in. He was a large, kind man.

Stephen's heart beat so loudly in his ears that he could hardly think. Had the captain heard the code? No, he couldn't have heard them from behind the thick library door! The soldier had only whispered.

Seeing the captain, the regular snapped to his feet in attention. The captain waved a pudgy hand. "Sit down. Heard the bells ring when you came in." He studied the soldier's hand. "Nasty wound there."

"I looked for the troop's doctor. When I couldn't find him, I came here."

Stephen stood up. "I can take care of it, sir."

The captain looked down his thick nose into Stephen's eyes. "I shouldn't be surprised if you can. The doctor speaks highly of you, lad."

Stephen grinned with pride. "Thank you, sir."

"Show the other officers to the library when they arrive, will you? There's a good lad."

When the library door shut behind the captain, Stephen wondered what to do next. Should he repeat the code, so the deserter would know he'd found the right man?

But what if he wasn't the deserter? What if the redcoats had found out about the plan and this man was here to trap him?

Stephen rubbed sweaty palms down the thighs of his wool homespun breeches. "I'm going to get a needle and take a couple stitches so your wound will heal faster."

While he threaded the curved needle, his mind raced. He could play it safe. He could pretend the man's words meant nothing to him. But if he was a deserter and Stephen didn't help him, would he ever have another chance to get away?

The man held his wounded hand in the candlelight while Stephen bent his head over the wound and made his stitches. When he was done, while their heads were still close together above the tin lantern, he whispered, "God bless the Liberty Boys."

Liberty, who had been sleeping in a ball beneath the table, sat up, thudded his skinny tail against the floor, and whined.

Stephen chuckled. "Not you, boy." He explained to the soldier about Liberty's name.

The soldier's face lit up in a smile. He patted Liberty's head. "Thought I'd made a mistake when you didn't repeat the code." They both talked in whispers.

"Are you going to come back after the officers go to bed?" Stephen asked.

The soldier shook his head. "I'm not leaving. When it's discovered I'm missing, the officers will remember I was here. They'll know I was hurt. They won't think you or this place have anything to do with my escape."

Stephen led the soldier over to the waist-high wooden counter and opened two doors beneath the counter. Then he looked the soldier up and down. He wasn't a tall man—he was about Stephen's height. He wasn't large or fat, either, but he had broad shoulders.

"I thought this would be the perfect place to hide you," Stephen whispered. "Some doctors' apprentices sleep on shelves in doctors' apothecaries. But I'm not sure you'll fit."

Stephen had emptied the cupboard earlier. He'd even taken out the middle shelf to make more room.

The soldier squatted down and held the lantern by the tin handle at the top so it shone into the cupboard. "A bit of a tight squeeze, perhaps, but I think I can make it."

He stood, set the lantern down, and held out his good hand. "Thank you, Stephen Lankford. I'll never forget the chance you're taking for me. My name is George Smythe. I hope we'll meet again someday, when the redcoats have left Boston."

"My ancestors were named Smythe. They came to America from England in 1620, over 150 years ago."

Mr. Smythe grinned. "Maybe we're related."

It was a new thought to Stephen that any of the soldiers in Boston might be related to him.

"Go open the door, Stephen, and pretend I'm leaving."

Stephen did as he was told. He glanced up and down the street to see whether there was anyone that might see him. He saw only a couple lantern flickers too far away for the people carrying them to tell whether anyone stood before the apothecary. In a loud voice, he wished Mr. Smythe godspeed, and told him to come back in a couple days to have the doctor look at his wound. Then he hurried back to the counter. He pointed to a cloth bag in the cupboard. "Your new clothes are in there."

"Daren't change now. I'd better try out my new home before the officers come out here." Smythe grinned.

Laughing voices outside the door startled them. Smythe scuttled into the cupboard, drawing his knees up beneath his chin. Stephen closed the doors just as Lieutenant Rand and Anna entered.

Stephen bit his bottom lip hard. If there was anyone he *didn't* want to see, it was Lieutenant Rand! No one would rather catch a Lankford with a deserter than that man.

Lieutenant Rand was carrying a tray with pewter mugs and a tall bottle. Anna carried a large silver bowl with oranges, lemons, and spices in it. She wore an ankle-length cape over her warm quilted skirt to keep away the November chill.

"Why, Stephen, I thought you'd be home by now!" Anna set her bowl beside the lantern on the cupboard. "Lieutenant

Rand stopped by the house to visit his friends, but they'd already come here. So he helped me carry these things over. The officers always like some punch in the evenings."

Lieutenant Rand set the tray beside the bowl. "Working late?"

"Yes. I'm still cleaning up." A movement across the room caught his attention. Liberty was playing with Mr. Smythe's hat!

Stephen's feet seemed to freeze to the floor. What if Rand saw that redcoat hat? He mustn't!

Liberty and the hat were in the shadows. Rand might not recognize the hat if he didn't get close to it. But what if Liberty dragged it closer?

The best thing to do would be to go right over and pick up the hat, like nothing was wrong, he decided.

He almost had to pick his feet up with his hands to make them move, he was so scared. He untied his black apron as he walked. When he reached Liberty, the dog thumped his tail wildly, thinking Stephen was going to play.

Stephen dropped his apron on top of the hat, and picked them up together. Liberty caught one of the apron's ties in his teeth and growled playfully. "No! Down!" Stephen ordered.

Liberty tucked her head.

"You hurt his feelings," Anna said. "He just wants to play."

"Stupid mutt." Lieutenant Rand started toward the library. Liberty darted under a chair. The dog had learned that Lieutenant Rand's boots had a way of kicking him if he wasn't careful.

As Lieutenant Rand passed him, Stephen bundled the apron closer about the hat and shook his head. "Always cloths and aprons to wash out when you're a doctor's apprentice."

Lieutenant Rand made a face at the mention of the bloody apron and quickly entered the library.

Stephen breathed a sigh of relief. He'd never have gotten away with it if it had been daylight! At the counter, he opened the door, threw in the hat and apron, and slammed the door shut before Anna could see anything.

"Why are you putting dirty cloths in there?" Anna asked, removing her cloak. "You know Father doesn't like them in the cupboard."

"I'll take them with me when I go home."

They worked together making the punch. Stephen's mouth watered at the wonderful smells of the oranges and lemons when he sliced them.

"It's so nice having the officers quartered with us," Anna said. "They can get the best food. We can't afford fruit like this anymore."

Anna chattered away, but Stephen hardly heard her. All he could think about was the man in the cupboard beneath the punch bowl. Anna stepped to his side of the counter and reached for the cupboard door. Stephen's stomach did a somersault.

CHAPTER 12
Fighting Friends

Stephen slammed his hand flat against the cupboard's handle. Anna jumped back, her blue eyes wide. "Stephen, whatever is the matter with you?"

"I, um, I cleaned out the cupboards today and moved some things. What are you looking for? Maybe I can help you find it."

"I already asked you three times for the small tin grater Father keeps there. When you didn't get it for me, I decided to get it myself."

"Sorry, I didn't hear you. Guess I let my mind wander." He pulled open a nearby drawer and handed her the grater.

"Must be wandering the other side of Boston," she joked.

Captain Ingles came in from the library. "Bring us more firewood, lad. We plan to be here awhile."

Stephen hurried to get the wood, his heart sinking. Every minute the soldiers spent in the library was another minute of danger for the deserting soldier—and for Stephen!

An idea popped into his head. He'd spent three years learning from Dr. Cuyler how to use the many herbs in the apothecary. Could he use what he'd learned tonight? He was smiling when he set the logs beside the officers' fireplace.

While Anna scraped the hard brown nutmeg against the tin grater, Stephen ground some of Dr. Cuyler's herbs in a mortar.

"What's that?" Anna asked, when he poured the crushed herbs into the punch.

"Just something new."

"What if it makes the punch taste funny?"

"The officers will like it fine." The herb didn't have much taste. It made people sleepy. He'd had to use a lot of it in the punch. He hoped it would work and send the men home early to bed.

They carried the bowl and mugs into the library. Anna used a dipper to fill the mugs. Captain Ingles smacked his lips and reached for a poker heating in the fireplace. The poker sizzled when he stuck it in his mug to warm the spiced punch.

Lieutenant Rand picked up a mug. "At least there's one family in Boston that knows how to give an Englishman good food."

Stephen clenched his teeth. He knew Lieutenant Rand was reminding him that Kathleen wouldn't serve him English tea.

When Stephen went back to the apothecary, he was

alarmed to see Anna by the cupboard doors again. "What do you want?" he asked sharply.

She jumped, then plopped her fists on her hips and glared at him. "Stop barking at me like that, Stephen Lankford. I'm looking for a cloth to wipe up some punch the officers spilled.

Stephen found her a clean rag. She glared at him again when she grabbed the rag from him. When she walked into the library, Stephen leaned back against the wall and took a deep breath. What would Anna do if she opened the cupboard and found the soldier? Most likely she'd tell the officers right away! She'd think it was the right thing for an English citizen to do.

If she thought Stephen was helping Mr. Smythe, would she still tell the officers? Stephen didn't think so, but he wasn't sure. He'd just have to see that she *didn't* find Mr. Smythe!

He started rearranging books on a shelf near the library door. It was a good place to stand to try to overhear the officers, so he often pretended to be busy there.

"Bark! Bark!"

Stephen whirled around at Liberty's yelp. Liberty was usually too well behaved to bark inside!

Liberty was in front of the cupboard door. His nose was almost on the floor. His rear end, with its tail going a mile a minute, was stuck up in the air.

Something red on the floor in front of Liberty moved. A piece of Mr. Smythe's uniform! It must have fallen out when Anna had started opening the door. Smythe was trying to pull it back inside without opening the door.

Liberty jumped on the moving cloth with another yelp. He growled playfully, tugging the cloth back and forth.

"Did Liberty see a mouse?" Anna asked.

Stephen's heart leaped right into his throat at her unexpected voice. He hurried toward Liberty. "One of the dirty cloths must have fallen out of the cupboard. I'll get it."

She followed him, chuckling at Liberty's antics. Stephen wished she would go to another part of the room!

The library door opened. "Can't you keep that mutt quiet?" Lieutenant Rand bellowed.

"We're trying, sir," Stephen said. He knelt beside Liberty, hiding the piece of red cloth. If Lieutenant Rand saw the cloth, he'd be sure to know it was part of a redcoat's uniform!

"Dogs don't belong inside anyway," Rand muttered, closing the library door.

It wasn't easy to make Liberty let go of the cloth, but Stephen finally did. "Would you put Liberty outside for me?"

"It's cold out! Why can't he wait for us in here?"

"I don't want Lieutenant Rand to kick Liberty again."

Anna grabbed the leather tie Stephen kept around Liberty's neck. "I don't understand why Lieutenant Rand is so mean to Liberty. He's such a nice man in every other way."

He's only nice to you because you're not a Patriot, Stephen thought. When Anna and Liberty were at the shop door, he opened the cupboard door and pushed the piece of uniform at Mr. Smythe.

"Sorry," the soldier mouthed.

Stephen took the dirty cloths he'd put away in there earlier and closed the door. His heart still hadn't slowed down!

Liberty was whimpering outside the apothecary door. *Between Liberty and Anna, Mr. Smythe isn't very safe!* Stephen thought. "It's getting late. Why don't I walk you home, Anna? It will be a while before the officers leave, and I have to bank the fire. They won't miss me for a few minutes."

Anna yawned and reached for her cape hanging on a wooden peg beside the door. "I'll come for their dirty dishes in the morning."

Stephen took the tin lantern to light their way, leaving the apothecary in darkness. At the door, he looked back at where he knew the cupboard stood. Would the officers find Mr. Smythe while they were gone? He'd have to take the chance. It was safer than having Anna and Liberty around!

Mr. Smythe was still tucked away in the cupboard when Stephen returned. Anna had kept Liberty with her, much to Stephen's relief. The herbs must have worked, he thought, when the officers ended their evening earlier than usual. Stretching and yawning, they said good night to him on their way out.

When he'd shuttered the windows and barred the door so no one could surprise them, he opened the cupboard door. Mr. Smythe slipped quickly out of his uniform to change into his "new" clothes.

Stephen chuckled. "Hope you don't mind looking like a woman."

Mr. Smythe grinned. "Not if it gets me out of Boston safely."

Stephen helped Mr. Smythe into an old dress and petticoat of his mother's. A wig hid the man's brown curls. A lace-edged mobcap topped it all off.

Stephen stuffed the uniform into the cloth bag and hid it behind some pottery in another cupboard.

When it was almost dawn, Mr. Smythe shaved carefully with Will's razor. He put on an old hooded cloak, slid a market basket Stephen had brought over his arm, and slipped into the still dark street.

Stephen knew Mr. Smythe was to meet a Patriot farmer

at the market and leave Boston with him later that day. Would he make it? Or would the redcoats stop the funny-looking woman?

Captain Ingles asked Stephen about Mr. Smythe the next day. Had he said where he was going when he left the apothecary?

Stephen said, "Maybe he went to one of the taverns that are so popular with soldiers." At least he knew the man was still free! He was glad he'd buried the uniform in the herb garden early that morning.

Days later Will said, "The post rider says the package you sent arrived safely."

Stephen frowned. "The package?"

William grinned, nodded, and walked away.

"Oh!" The package was Mr. Smythe. If he "arrived safely," he must have made it out of Boston. Stephen wondered where he was living. Would he stay in another town in Massachusetts, or on a farm, or would he live in another colony, far away from the redcoats that might recognize him? Would they ever see each other again?

Stephen and Anna spent fall days in the medical garden, removing plants before they were killed by early winter frosts. In the apothecary, they tied the plants together in bunches and hung them upside down from the ceiling to dry. Soon the ceiling was covered with fragrant purple, yellow, and white flowers.

One morning while Stephen and Anna were tying up bunches of lavender thistle, the bell above the door jingled cheerfully and Anna's friend Sara entered.

Anna's face brightened. "Hello! I haven't seen you in days!"

"I've been busy." Sara fumbled with the red-and-white

checked material covering the basket on her arm.

Anna nodded. "Me, too. We've been cleaning the garden. Tomorrow I'm delivering food baskets to some invalids and older ladies for the Gifts Committee. Will you help me?"

Sara shook her head, her brown curls bouncing on the white linen scarf tied over the top of her blue dress. "I don't think so."

"But it would be fun! It would give us time to be together."

Sara lifted her head with a jerk. Her blue eyes flashed. "I said no!"

Anna gasped and stepped back.

Stephen stared, his hands clenched around thistle stems. He'd never heard Sara speak so sharply.

Sara hurried to the counter and set down her basket. "I need some medicine. Mother's teeth are hurting." Her chin lifted and she glared at Stephen. "We can't pay for it right now, but Father says to tell the doctor he'll pay for it as soon as the port opens again."

Stephen nodded, pretending it was normal for Sara's father to ask for credit. "Of course."

"I'll get the herbs." Anna took down a white china jar from a shelf.

"Is that the right medicine?" Sara asked Stephen.

"Yes," Stephen assured her. "Anna's learned a lot about herbs from her father. If women could be doctors, she'd make a good doctor one day."

Anna spooned a bit of herb onto a piece of paper. Then she folded the paper so none of the herb could fall out and tied a bit of string about it.

She handed the packet to Sara. "Pour hot water over these herbs, the same as if you were making tea. Then have your mother put the wet leaves on her teeth."

"Thank you," Sara mumbled, dropping the package into her basket. She hurried toward the door.

Anna shot Stephen a worried glance.

"Wait, Sara, please." Anna bit her bottom lip as if she didn't know what to say next. "I don't know what I've done to make you mad, but I'm sorry."

Sara started to walk around her without saying anything.

Anna grabbed her arm. "Please, Sara, tell me what's wrong."

"It's the Gifts Committee you help with. My family is using some of the food and firewood people have donated. I'm so. . .ashamed." Tears ran down her freckled cheeks.

Anna stared at her, openmouthed.

Stephen knew she didn't know what to say. She was probably as uncomfortable as he felt. He cleared his throat. "It's not your father's fault the king took away his job when the harbor closed. All the Patriots have to stick together and help each other through these hard times."

"Right now your family needs things other people can give them," Anna said. "Another time, your family will be helping someone. That's the way it works."

Sara blinked at her tears. "When the tea was thrown into the harbor and later when the port was closed and the Patriots were all saying they'd starve before they'd pay for the tea, it felt so brave to be a Patriot." She brushed a hand over her eyes and sniffed. "It doesn't feel brave when you're begging for food."

Anna rubbed a hand on Sara's arm. Stephen noticed Anna's eyes looked like they might have tears in them, too.

Sara jerked away from Anna's touch. "It's Loyalists like you who have made so much trouble for Boston."

"Us? *We* didn't throw the tea in the harbor!"

"You didn't stand up with us, either." Sara's voice jerked angrily. "If the Loyalists had stood by the Patriots, everything would have been fine. The king wouldn't have shut the harbor if everyone stood up to him together."

Anna stared at her. "Sara, that's silly."

"I don't want to be friends with you anymore, Anna Allerton. I only want Patriots for friends." Sara stormed out the door.

Anna turned to Stephen. "She isn't right, is she? It's not our fault."

"No, it's not your fault. She's just hurting and doesn't know what to do about it."

"Hurting me won't help."

"No." Stephen looked about the room. In all the jars of medicines and herbs, there was nothing that would help when friends hurt friends.

November moved into December. Days went along like usual, until one evening during the second week of December, when Stephen was again staying late at the apothecary shop while the officers played cards, smoked their long pipes, and visited.

He was trying to read a new medical book by candlelight, but his eyes kept closing. He wished the men would leave so he could go to bed. Then he heard words that wakened him like a clap of thunder: "Fort William and Mary."

On tiptoe, he moved to the closed library door and leaned his ear against it. He held his breath so he could hear better. What he heard set his mind whirling. British troops were being sent from Boston to Fort William and Mary in New Hampshire!

William and the Observers needed this news right away! Stephen took one step toward the front door. He stopped; the officers would think it strange if he left for long.

Chairs scraping against the library floor sent him dashing back to his chair. He dropped his head and arms on his open book and closed his eyes.

Officers filed into the room, joking with each other. Stephen's heart raced. He was breathing as hard as if he'd just raced back from the Neck. He made himself breathe slowly and deeply, as if he were sleeping.

Boots stopped beside him. A thick hand grasped his shoulder. "Time to wake up, lad." Captain Ingles shook him.

Stephen blinked, sat up, and looked at the officers. He stretched his arms over his head. "Leaving?"

"Yes, lad," the captain answered. "Ye'd best see to banking the fireplace."

Stephen pretended to yawn. "See you tomorrow night." He stumbled toward the library while the officers left. He made quick work of banking the fireplace and snuffing the candles. Even with such an important message to deliver, he didn't dare leave the fire and candles burning with no one in the shop.

Snow and ice made it hard to hurry along the dark, narrow streets. Only the moon and stars lit his way. A lantern might have been seen by soldiers or others. He didn't want anyone to remember seeing him on the street so late at night. Not when he was carrying an important Patriot secret!

His own house was dark and quiet when he reached it. The family was already in bed. He lit the candle on the hall table and carried it with him so he wouldn't fall and make noise. He didn't want to wake Lieutenant Andrews or Lieutenant Rand!

His mind kept saying "Hurry! Hurry!" but he walked slowly. He tried to remember which steps and which floorboards squeaked.

Creak! He stopped. His heart slammed against his chest. He'd forgotten about the board right in front of William's door! Had anyone heard him? No one stirred. He slowly opened Will's door.

When he woke Will, he held the candle high so Will could see him and put his finger to his lips.

Stephen whispered in Will's ear that he had news he must tell him right away.

"Kitchen," Will whispered back.

Together they went downstairs, stepping over the squeaky places. When they reached the kitchen, Will opened the barrel of apple cider beside the back door. Taking the tin ladle hanging on the wall, he dipped the cool cider into two pewter mugs.

He handed a mug to Stephen. "If anyone walks in, we'll say I woke up thirsty. I came down for a drink and met you coming in."

"I know you said we aren't to tell Patriot news in the house, but this is too important to wait until morning," Stephen whispered.

They stood close together beside the fireplace, where they could still feel a little heat from the banked ashes. Stephen shivered from the eerie sound his and Will's whispers made in the large, dark room.

"What's your news?" William asked.

Stephen told how he'd overheard the officers. "General Gage is sending redcoats from Boston to Fort William and

Mary at Portsmouth, New Hampshire. They'll go by sea."

"Why?"

"There's only a few redcoats at the fort. General Gage wants more soldiers there in case the minutemen try to take the fort's gunpowder."

In the light of the candle Stephen had set on the mantle, he could see excitement dancing in Will's eyes. "The minutemen must get the gunpowder before the soldiers from Boston arrive."

"To do that, they'd have to go into the fort and take the powder from under the redcoats' noses," Stephen said.

"Yes."

"But if the soldiers catch them, they might be shot."

"Yes." Will agreed.

"I mean," Stephen tried to explain his worst fears, "if the redcoats and minutemen shoot at each other, war could start."

"Yes. Mark my words, if General Gage keeps taking Americans' guns and ammunition to use against us, war will surely start. If not at Fort William and Mary, then somewhere else."

Hopelessness filled Stephen's chest. He didn't want war. He wanted peace with the king and his troops. Like most Patriots, he only wanted the king to let Massachusetts be ruled by the old charter, the same charter granted to Massachusetts by King William and Queen Mary, for whom the fort was named.

"If this news gets to the minutemen," Stephen said slowly, "then *I* could start the war, because it's my secret."

Will's fingers squeezed Stephen's shoulder tightly through the wool jacket. "This might be the most important news the Sons of Liberty have discovered. The Patriots must hear it."

"I thought the Continental Congress said the Patriots' army wasn't to shoot at the redcoats unless the redcoats shot first."

"That's right. But if the redcoats take all our ammunition, we won't be able to fight. We'll have to do whatever the king says, no matter how wrong it is."

Stephen nodded slowly. He hadn't thought of that.

Will rubbed a fist across his stubbly chin. "We need to tell Paul Revere. Portsmouth is sixty miles north, and the roads are covered with snow and ice. Paul's the only man we can count on to get through in time."

Stephen swallowed hard. "Do. . .do you want me to tell him?" Would he have to sneak into Mr. Revere's house tonight?

Will shook his head, his brown hair brushing his shoulders. "No, it's too dangerous. If you were caught entering Paul's house, the British might become suspicious. Mark my words, when they find the Portsmouth minutemen know the redcoats are being sent from Boston, General Gage will try to find how the news got out. We don't want anyone to remember you were at Dr. Cuyler's and at Paul's house the same night."

Stephen yawned and picked up the wool blanket that was folded neatly at one end of the tall-backed settle. Now that he'd passed the news and worry on to Will, he was tired again! "I'm going to bed."

Will grabbed his arm as he started to lay down on the settle. "Oh, no, you don't. You need to go back to Dr. Cuyler's and sleep in the library. No one must know you came home tonight. We don't want anyone to think you had a chance to tell Father and me what the officers said."

Stephen sighed. He didn't want to go out in the cold and snow again, but Will was right. He slipped quietly out the back door while Will went to dress.

CHAPTER 13
The Raid

Will got the message safely to Mr. Revere. Stephen wondered what Mr. Revere said to get out of town. General Gage didn't let people into or out of Boston without a pass anymore. To get a pass, you had to have a good reason to leave. Stephen smiled at the thought of Paul Revere saying, "I'm off to warn the minutemen that you're sending soldiers to Fort William and Mary." No, Mr. Revere would have come up with another reason.

Three days later Paul Revere was back. Stephen was surprised he'd made the dangerous ride so quickly. Every day he was gone, Stephen had prayed that Mr. Revere would be safe, the message would get through, and war wouldn't start.

Mr. Revere told Will what happened at Fort William and Mary. Will and Father printed the news in the *Boston Observer*.

Paul Revere had reached the minutemen before the soldiers from Boston arrived at the fort. In the middle of the night, the minutemen went to the fort in Portsmouth Harbor in boats. The British captain in charge of the fort fired three times at the minutemen, but hit no one. The captain knew he didn't have enough soldiers at the fort to win a battle, so he surrendered.

Patriots, Loyalists, and redcoats in Boston were all shocked when they heard the news. Minutemen had taken a British fort without anyone on either side wounded or killed!

Will grinned when he told Stephen the news. "The minutemen carried away ninety-seven kegs of gunpowder and about one hundred guns and hid them. The minutemen need those guns and ammunition. They wouldn't have them without you."

Stephen couldn't help but be proud as he heard the town talk about the minutemen's raid. Lieutenant Rand and Lieutenant Andrews told the family that General Gage was mad that news of his plans had leaked out.

Mr. Revere made Stephen a gift: a small silver whistle shaped like a spy glass with the words "Boston Observer" carved on the side. Stephen carried it with him everywhere. He'd stick his hand in his breeches' pocket, feel the satiny smooth silver, and smile at the memory of Mr. Revere's and Will's praise.

He showed his whistle to Anna and his friends. He would have loved to brag to them why he had the whistle, but he didn't. Only Mr. Revere, Will, and Stephen would ever know that "Boston Observer" didn't refer to the name of his father's newspaper, but to his work as a spy for the secret Observers group.

Anna didn't like the news about Fort William and Mary one bit. She was at the apothecary when Stephen told her what had happened at the fort—without telling her his part in it. She set the blue bottle she was dusting back on the shelf with a thud. "The minutemen must have known General Gage was sending soldiers to the fort."

"I suppose so." Stephen was checking the wooden medicine box Dr. Cuyler kept in the trunk on the back of his carriage. It was his chore to keep the box stocked with twine, splints, bandages, sponges, medicines, and things to make pills and powders.

The feathers in Anna's duster fluttered over a row of large jars with curving blue letters. "A spy must have told them."

Stephen's heart lurched against his chest. He opened his mouth but couldn't say anything.

"Maybe one of his own soldiers," she said. "I think it's awful, a British soldier betraying his country."

"Maybe it wasn't a soldier," Stephen said, watching her closely. "Maybe it was a Patriot who overheard the plans."

Anna picked up a small metal scale in one hand, dusted the cupboard beneath it, and slammed it back down with a crash. "Citizens shouldn't betray their country, either."

"Surely whoever told thought it was the right thing to do."

"The Patriots always think they're doing the right thing, but look what a mess they've made of Boston and of our lives!"

Stephen shifted his shoulders uncomfortably. "They haven't done anything but ask the king to put things between England and the colonies back the way they were years ago, before the Stamp Act and the Tea Act, and—"

"They haven't done anything?" she interrupted him. "They've done *everything!* It's because of them the harbor is closed. I'm tired of making do with whatever food we can get. I want sugar and molasses instead of dried pumpkin for baking. I want new clothes." She held out her quilted skirt. "Look at this old thing! I've mended a dozen holes in it this winter, and it's too short. I'd be able to buy a new dress if the port opened."

"But Anna—"

"I'm tired of sharing my house with strangers, too. I'm tired of our families arguing. Remember the fun our families used to have together? Now our fathers don't even talk to each other!"

"That's not the Patriots' fault."

"Everything is the Patriots' fault!" She stamped her small slippered foot on the wooden floor.

"Even your father says the king is punishing Boston more than is fair," he reminded her.

"I don't care. If I knew who the spy was that told General Gage's plans for Fort William and Mary, I'd turn him in myself."

The marble pestle Stephen had been holding hit the countertop and rolled onto the floor. "You don't mean it! The spy could be someone you know, maybe a good friend."

She picked up the pestle and slammed it down on the counter. Her blue eyes were almost black with anger. "Spies make things worse. I want life to go back to the way it used to be."

"Turning against our neighbors isn't the answer."

Anna tugged at her lace-trimmed mobcap. "You're a

Patriot, but you also believe in doing what's right. Wouldn't you turn in a spy?"

"Maybe not, if he was someone I knew."

"You're just as stubborn as your father, Stephen Lankford! You don't do awful things like the rebels who threw the tea in the harbor, but you're a Patriot just the same. Can't you see that all of you Patriots are hurting Boston?"

"I don't believe that."

Anna tossed her feather duster on the counter. She crossed to the wall pegs beside the door and threw her long gray cape over her shoulders. "I don't want to be around you anymore."

"Anna, come back!" Stephen called as she stormed out the door, letting in a blast of wintry wind.

She kept walking.

Feelings grew worse between Anna and Stephen throughout the winter. Anna didn't talk to him anymore. When she came to the shop, she ignored him. She didn't look at him or smile at him. At first he missed her friendship. He hated having her angry with him. Then he got tired of hurting and let himself be angry with her instead.

Feelings grew worse between the redcoats and Patriots during the winter, too. The redcoats were afraid the Charles River would freeze over and that the minutemen would cross the ice to attack the troops.

But the river didn't freeze over. It was a mild winter, which was good for everyone in Boston. Fuel was scarce. A colder winter would have meant the poor people would have suffered more. The Patriots were sure God made the winter mild to help them.

Hopes for peace grew dimmer. The Patriots were preparing more and more for war. Patriot gunmakers were busy in all the colonies, making muskets for the minutemen. Paul Revere and other silversmiths made bullet molds. Stephen's mother, Will's wife, and other Patriot women gave their silver and pewter dishes and candlesticks to be melted down and made into bullets. Stephen wondered if Lieutenant Andrews and Lieutenant Rand noticed the dishes and candlesticks missing from his house.

Dan came to town often, bringing things to market. He always stopped by to visit Stephen. He told how he and his father spent their evenings in front of the family fireplace carving wooden bowls and spoons the minutemen would need if war came.

Stephen was glad there'd been no fighting between the redcoats and minutemen. So far, the only people killed had been British deserters who had been caught and shot at the common. Each time it happened, Stephen thought of Mr. Smythe. Where was he? Was he safe?

In February, General Gage's men tried to take the ammunition stored at Salem. It was then that Will told Stephen that Mr. Smythe, the deserter he'd helped escape, was living near Salem. He was helping train the minutemen.

The Observers hadn't been able to get a message to Salem. General Gage had locked Paul Revere, Will, and some of their friends in jail at the fort on Castle Island to keep them from telling Salem. So now the Observers knew that the general had his own spy in the Observers.

Even without the Observers, Gage's men weren't able to take Salem's ammunition.

March fifth was the fifth anniversary of the Boston Massacre.

People gathered at Old South Church to remember those who'd lost their lives in the massacre.

The building was packed. People were crushed together in the pews. The aisles were filled. Men even stood on the two-foot-deep windowsills. Stephen knew the streets were crowded, too. Thousands had turned out.

Stephen glanced up at the balcony and saw Anna and Dr. Cuyler. They sat where young Josiah Quincy had been the night of the tea party. Stephen could still remember his chilling words that night. "I see the clouds which now rise thick and fast upon our horizon. . .to that God who rides the whirlwind and directs the storm I commit my country." How close was the storm of war?

Stephen looked at the front of the church and laughed. Dr. Warren, the Patriot leader, was climbing into the church through the window above the high pulpit! He hadn't been able to make it through the crowd.

It was Dr. Warren who had written the Suffolk Resolves that Stephen and Will had printed and Paul Revere had carried to the Continental Congress at Philadelphia last summer. Dr. Warren had come to the print shop to thank Stephen's father for doing such a quick, good print job.

Wealthy John Hancock, who had been the leader of the Continental Congress, and Sam Adams, one of the smartest Patriot leaders, were beside Dr. Warren.

Forty British officers took the best pews at the front of the church and sat on the steps that led to the high pulpit. Stephen and Will exchanged worried glances. There was a rumor that General Gage was going to arrest the Patriot leaders today. The Loyalists had even made up a song about hanging them.

The redcoats couldn't frighten the Patriot leaders from

speaking. Dr. Warren told the story of the Boston Massacre. He reminded the people of all the reasons they were proud to be English citizens.

"It isn't our aim to become a separate country from Great Britain," he said. "Our wish is that Britain and the colonies grow stronger together. But if our peaceful attempts aren't successful, and the only way to safety lies through war, I know you will not turn your faces from the enemy."

The soldiers jeered. The crowd cheered.

Out in the street after the meeting, Stephen stopped to talk to Dr. Cuyler. The crowd about them parted to let Sam Adams and John Hancock through. Stephen saw Anna's icy blue glare as the men walked past. He knew she hadn't changed her mind about Patriots.

No one had been arrested at the meeting after all. Was it because the soldiers were afraid the crowd would turn on the redcoats if they arrested the popular leaders?

Stephen thought the leaders must have been frightened, even though they weren't arrested. In the days that followed, the Patriot leaders quietly slipped out of town, one by one, until only Dr. Warren was left.

The thunder of war sounded louder than ever.

CHAPTER 14

Danger for the Lankfords

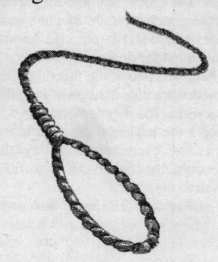

Stephen smiled as he entered the printing shop. It was mid-April, and the air outside was filled with the chatter of birds and the smell of cherry blossoms. The shop still smelled like ink. His father always said ink was his favorite smell, because ink printed words, and words were man's most powerful tools, next to faith in God.

After Will and Father had greeted Stephen, Will handed him a freshly printed newspaper. "Read what Patrick Henry said."

Stephen read it aloud. "We have done everything that could be done to stop the storm from coming. There is no longer any room for hope of peace. If we want to keep those rights for which we've been struggling for ten long years, we must fight!

"We shall not fight our battles alone. There is a just God, who rules nations. He will raise up friends to fight our battles for us.

"Is life so dear or peace so sweet as to be bought at the price of slavery? Forbid it, Almighty God. I know not what course others may take, but as for me, give me liberty or give me death!"

Stephen stared at the shaking paper in his hands. No, it was his hands that shook! Prickles ran up and down his spine.

"Do you think he's right?" he asked. "Do you think we'll have to fight?"

"I think he's right," his father said.

William nodded.

Stephen walked outside. The sun still shone, warming the cobblestones. Redcoats, tradesmen, and housewives coming from market still filled the street. Idle craftsmen still sat on barrels and benches, visiting. Birds still chattered and cherry blossoms still perfumed the air.

But nothing was the same.

The next day, Stephen saw people all over town reading the *Boston Observer* and heard them repeating Patrick Henry's words.

After work, Stephen hurried to his father's shop, with Liberty at his heels. He'd just arrived when a clattering in the street drew him and his father to the door. Stephen couldn't believe what he saw.

Lieutenant Rand and three other officers were riding their horses through the street. A large group of soldiers followed on foot, calling insults at the Patriots and laughing. Rand carried a large straw man. There was a grin on the lieutenant's face that made Stephen's skin crawl.

People in the street hurried to get out of the horses' paths. Then they stopped and watched to see where the soldiers were going. Everyone knew what the straw man was for.

So did Stephen. He'd seen others often enough.

The officers pulled their horses to a stop in front of the shop. Rand leaped off his horse. He grinned at Stephen and his father when he and one of the other officers stopped a foot in front of them. Liberty growled deep in his throat, peeking at Rand from behind Stephen's legs.

People in the street drew nearer, but Stephen knew they couldn't stop the redcoats.

The other officer carried a rope with a noose at one end. He tossed the other end over the shop sign's metal pole, then hooked the noose over the straw man.

Stephen's stomach tightened when they pulled the straw man up, letting it swing in the breeze. He knew what they were doing. It was called hanging someone in effigy. They were pretending to hang his father.

A copy of the *Boston Observer* was pinned to one straw hand. Rand grabbed a pipe from a nearby shopkeeper. He held it beneath the paper until it started on fire.

Liberty yelped and scuttled away.

Stephen darted into the shop. He grabbed the bucket of water that always stood beside the press. The straw would go up like kindling and could start the building on fire! Water sloshed over the floor and his shoes as he raced to the door. The straw man was already one huge flame. The officers and his father had backed away.

Stephen tossed the entire bucket on the burning form. Most of the fire went out in a *hiss* of smoke. The rope continued to burn, scorching the wooden shop sign.

Mr. Lankford grabbed his composing stick, stuck it through the noose, and yanked the rope down. He stamped the flames out until only a smoking black circle remained.

Lieutenant Rand sat astride his bay horse and watched. Finally he leaned over the horse's neck. "Patrick Henry may not be afraid of war, but you should be, Mr. Lankford. If war breaks out, the treasonous printers will be among the first prisoners of war." He yanked at the reins, turned his horse, and galloped up the street, hooves clattering against the cobbles.

Stephen's fists curled into balls. "I *hate* that man!"

His father's arm slid around his shoulders. "We're to love our enemies, son. He needs our prayers, not our hate."

"Aren't we supposed to love everyone, not just our enemies?" Stephen asked.

"Yes, but it's hardest to be nice to our enemies."

"If that's true, why are you nicer to Lieutenant Rand than to Dr. Cuyler?" Stephen stormed into the street, his wet shoes slapping against the cobblestones.

Stephen was glad the next morning when Dr. Cuyler asked him to work in the medical garden. It felt good to be outside in the sunlight with the birds singing and the smell of fresh earth. His anger over Lieutenant Rand's straw man lightened a little as he worked, loosening the soil with his wooden rake.

The medical garden was more important than ever since the harbor had closed. Now when Dr. Cuyler ran out of medicines and herbs, it was difficult and expensive to replace them unless he could get them from the garden.

Stephen wasn't surprised to see Anna enter the medical garden. She often helped there and in the apothecary, even though they didn't speak to each other any longer.

A red plaid apron protected her skirt and long, loose blue blouse. Blue ribbons attached to the top of her huge round straw hat tied beneath her chin, pulling the sides of the hat down over her cheeks. The hat shone golden in the morning sunlight.

He *was* surprised when she stopped beside him, licking her lips nervously. He leaned on the end of his wooden rake, waiting for her to speak.

"I heard what happened at the print shop, Stephen. I. . .I'm sorry."

"I didn't think you cared what happened to me and my family anymore."

"Of course I care!" She took a deep breath. "I couldn't stand it if anything happened to your father and Will. You must have been awfully frightened yesterday."

"Not so much." He shrugged. "Well, maybe a little."

The sound of fifes and drums playing a British march drowned out the songs of birds in the nearby trees. Stephen and Anna moved to the white picket fence surrounding the garden to watch a regiment of redcoats parade past. Brass buttons and musket barrels flashed in the sun.

Six young Patriot boys followed along singing "Yankee Doodle" at the top of their lungs.

"When the British troops came to Boston, I thought everything would get better," Anna said. "Instead, everything got worse."

She leaned against the fence. "Maybe I was wrong blaming *everything* on the Patriots. Sara blames everything on the Loyalists, and I know that we aren't to blame for everything that's wrong."

"Are you two friends again?"

She shook her head. "No. Sara says she hates Loyalists and won't be friends with me anymore."

"I'm sorry, Anna."

"I always thought everything would work out between Britain and the colonies. But if Sara can hate me for being a Loyalist, and our fathers can stop talking to each other, and you and I can get so angry with each other, maybe Britain and the colonies will stay angry, too."

"Maybe."

"I don't want to be angry with you anymore, Stephen. I want us to be friends."

"I want that, too."

"Maybe if we remember the things we like about each other instead of our differences, we can stay friends forever. Do you think we could?"

"I hope so."

Anna wrapped her fingers around the top of a picket in the fence and watched the troops disappearing down the street. "Everyone in Boston seems angry these days. People keep talking about war. Sometimes, Stephen, I'm so scared."

He put a hand on her shoulder, wishing he knew what to

say to make her feel better. But the thought of war scared him, too.

The next evening Dr. Cuyler sent Stephen to his father with a message to meet him after dark at the print shop. Stephen did, but the secret meeting made him uneasy. It was so unlike his uncle.

Stephen, his father, and Will pretended to go to bed early that night. They said goodnight to the family and officers. Then they sneaked out an upstairs window.

When they reached the print shop, Dr. Cuyler stepped out of a shadow and joined them. Father made sure the wooden shutters were closed over the windows. Inside, Will lit a single candle from a warm coal in the banked fireplace. In the wavering light of the candle, the three Lankfords faced Dr. Cuyler.

Stephen's father crossed his arms over his chest. "You haven't spoken to me for six months, Cuyler. Now you order me and my sons to the print shop in the dark of night. Why?"

"General Gage is planning to take your press and arrest you for treason."

"No!" Stephen yelled. "It's not true!" He couldn't bear it to be true! His father and brother *couldn't* be arrested!

He felt his father's hand on his shoulder. "Quiet, son. How do you know this, Cuyler?"

Dr. Cuyler hesitated a moment. "An officer I trust told me. He knows my sister is your wife."

"Why arrest us now?" William asked.

"A ship arrived this week from England with a letter from the king to General Gage. The king told him to be tougher on the Patriots," Dr. Cuyler said. "You and your father need to leave town."

"Gage won't give us a pass out of town when he wants to arrest us," Father said. "Maybe Will or I could sneak out of town, but how could we sneak both our families out?"

Sweat trickled down Stephen's spine. He remembered the deserter he and Dan had seen captured at the gate. Would that happen to Will and his father?

"I've been thinking about this for hours," Dr. Cuyler said. "General Gage won't hurt your families. It's you and Will he wants. I promise to watch out for your families until you can return or they can join you. Because I'm a Loyalist doctor, I have a pass that lets me enter and leave Boston freely. The guards at the Neck see me so often that they don't even search me. I can sneak you out in my carriage."

Will grinned. "That's a great idea!"

Relief poured through Stephen. It was the perfect plan!

"No." Father shook his head and crossed his arms over his large chest. "I won't let you put yourself in danger. The officers at our house would quickly find we'd left town. When they found you'd left town the same night, you'd be arrested."

Dr. Cuyler's arms swung wide. "What else can you do?"

"We can find a way out of Boston ourselves." Father raised his eyebrows and looked at Will. "Can't we?"

Stephen knew he was asking Will whether he could get them out the same way Will had helped other deserters out of Boston.

Will nodded. "We'll find a way."

"If you can't find another way out," Dr. Cuyler said, "promise you'll let me help you."

"I promise. I'll never forget this, Cuyler, not the warning or the offer to put yourself in danger to help us."

Stephen thought the candlelight reflected off unshed tears

121

in his father's eyes. A moment later he decided he must have been wrong. He'd never seen his father cry.

Father cleared his throat. "Stephen said something to me yesterday that's been bothering me ever since."

Stephen looked at him in surprise. What had he said?

"He said he didn't understand why we were nicer to our enemies than to you, Cuyler." Stephen's father held out his huge, ink-stained hand. "Our families have worked together for over 150 years to build America. I'd like us to be friends, in spite of our differences. I'm asking you to forgive me."

Slowly, Dr. Cuyler took his hand. "Me, too."

"You told me often that God says we're to pray for our leaders," Father said. "Maybe that's a good place to start over."

"For King George III?" Dr. Cuyler asked.

"Yes, and the Patriot leaders."

"Oh, all right." Dr. Cuyler grinned. "I guess they can all use the Lord's help. I only hope it's not too late for peace."

"If war comes," Will said, "the leaders of both sides will need the Lord's help more than ever."

The four joined hands in the middle of the dark room. They prayed for wisdom for King George and the Patriot leaders and for peace in America.

After Dr. Cuyler left, Father put a hand on each of his sons' shoulders. "We've printed only what we believed was right. We have to trust that God will make a way of escape for us."

Will left to talk to friends in the Sons of Liberty who could help them find that way of escape. Stephen and his father began taking apart the press. "We make our living by it," Father said. "We can't let it be destroyed."

Will returned an hour later, the escape arranged. "Tomorrow is Easter. The soldiers won't dare arrest us until after church. That will give us time to say good-bye to our families."

Will had brought a two-wheeled wooden cart with him with three-foot-high sides. He put it in the alley behind the shop below a window. The alley was barely wider than the cart. Tall brick shops and homes lined both sides of the alley.

The three worked together, quietly loading the pieces of the heavy press into the cart. It was almost dawn when they were done. Will covered the cart with a dirty cotton tarp and took it to a friend who would hide it for them.

After church the next day, Father and Will told the other family members and Lieutenant Andrews, who always joined them for services, that they wanted to check something at the shop before lunch. Stephen and his mother and sisters walked home with smiles on their faces. They didn't want Lieutenant Andrews or anyone else to see how frightened they were.

Would William and Father escape? When would their family be together again?

Stephen prayed all the way home.

CHAPTER 15

Will Anna Tell?

By Tuesday evening, Stephen and his family still hadn't heard whether his father and Will were safe. "They must be," Stephen told himself. "If they'd been caught, the soldiers would have told us."

Lieutenant Rand would have loved to have given him the

bad news. The officer had been furious when he'd found they'd left town. He must have known General Gage was planning to arrest them, Stephen thought.

When Stephen stepped through the front door of his home, he heard a man's voice he didn't know coming through the closed sitting room door. The next voice he knew: Lieutenant Rand's. He leaned his ear against the door, listening.

The voice he didn't know was speaking. "You and Lieutenant Andrews are to report to the common as soon as possible, prepared for an expedition."

"Lieutenant Andrews isn't here," Lieutenant Rand said, "but I'll get the message to him."

Stephen stepped quickly from the doorway. Opening the front door, he pretended he was just entering the house as Lieutenant Rand and a soldier came out of the sitting room.

The soldier nodded at Stephen and left. Lieutenant Rand frowned at Stephen. "Do you know where Lieutenant Andrews is?"

"I haven't seen him, sir."

Rand grabbed his hat from the hallway table. "I'm going looking for him. If he gets back before I do, tell him to wait for me here."

Stephen watched him hurry down the street in his red coat and black hat. The officers were to be "prepared for an expedition," the soldier had said. That meant General Gage was sending his soldiers out of Boston, likely to take another town's gunpowder. He should tell Paul Revere, Stephen thought, but how many men was Gage sending, and where?

He worried about it for fifteen minutes, pacing back and forth in front of the fireplace. He could hear women's voices in the kitchen. His mother and sisters must be making supper.

He didn't talk to them. He had to figure out what he should do.

When Lieutenant Andrews walked in, Kathleen was with him. Her hand was tucked into the crook of his elbow.

"Lieutenant Rand is looking for you, sir," Stephen said. He almost blurted out that he was to go to the common but remembered just in time that he wasn't supposed to know that!

Lieutenant Andrews didn't answer. Instead he looked at Kathleen. Their faces were filled with worry.

The officer removed his hat and turned to Stephen. "While we were walking by the common, an officer stopped us. I'm to report there right away."

So he'd already heard the message.

Kathleen said, "Boats are waiting by the common to take soldiers across the river." She glanced at Lieutenant Andrews and back to Stephen. "It's not a secret. Anyone from town who goes to the common can see what's happening."

"Is it a secret where the troops are going?" Stephen asked.

"Yes." Lieutenant Andrews played with his hat and bit the corner of his bottom lip as if he couldn't decide whether to say more.

"They're going to try to take more of our ammunition, I suppose," Stephen said.

Lieutenant Andrews took Kathleen's hand. "When I came to America, I expected only to follow my orders and serve the king. I didn't expect to meet Kathleen or find I agree with the Patriots' beliefs. I didn't think I would ever betray my king and fellow soldiers, but to do otherwise would be to betray my conscience."

Stephen waited, his heart beating faster and faster.

The officer took a deep breath. "It's rumored we're going to Concord, on the other side of Lexington. Maybe we are to take the Americans' arms there in obedience to King George's recent orders. You must warn the Sons of Liberty, Stephen."

"Oh!"

At the gasp behind them, the three whirled around. Anna stood there, her hands to her cheeks, her eyes filled with horror. She must have been in the kitchen with his mother and sister, Stephen realized.

His feet felt rooted to the floor. Anna had told him she'd turn in a spy who was her friend without any pity. Would she turn in Lieutenant Andrews? Would she tell General Gage that Stephen was warning the Sons of Liberty?

Anna rushed across the floor, her soft slippers making little noise on the carpet. She stopped right in front of Lieutenant Andrews. She was a foot shorter than him, but she tilted up her chin and glared into his face.

"You are the worst kind of a coward, Lieutenant Andrews! If you want to be a Patriot, it would be much braver to desert and join them boldly."

She whirled around, her skirt a swirl of green. "As for you, Stephen Lankford, I came to tell you I'm sorry about your father and Will. I wanted us to be friends again."

"I want that, too," Stephen said.

Tears filled her eyes, but her chin jutted out the way it always did when she was angry. "You *can't* tell the Sons of Liberty the soldiers are marching. What if they fire on the soldiers, on our king's own troops?"

Her words made Stephen's chest hurt. She was at least partly right. If the minutemen knew the soldiers were coming, they'd get their guns and stand up to them. "The minutemen won't fire unless the redcoats fire first." At least that's what the

Patriots always said. He hoped it was true.

Anna's hands balled into fists at her sides. "Please don't tell, Stephen. How can we be friends if you tell?"

Stephen swallowed a lump in his throat. "Will you. . .will you tell General Gage if I do? Will you tell him about me and about Lieutenant Andrews?"

If she did, Stephen might be thrown in prison, but Lieutenant Andrews would be tried as a traitor and might be killed.

Her hands opened and closed at her sides. "If I tell about Lieutenant Andrews, I'll have to tell about you."

No one said anything for a long minute.

"No, I won't tell!" she yelled. "What can the minutemen do to the king's troops? The minutemen are nothing but pests to the redcoats! Telling your secret won't help the Patriots at all!"

"Thank you, Anna," he said quietly.

"Just go away!" she screamed.

He ran out of the house, headed for Paul Revere's house. He didn't know who else to tell.

His thoughts were on Anna as he ran. If she'd turned him in, the family would have been torn apart by her choice. Yet her loyalty to the king was so strong. It must have been hard for her to spare him and Lieutenant Andrews. He knew she'd always wonder if she'd done the right thing.

He banged on the door of Mr. Revere's house in North Square. The streets were filled with redcoats dressed for battle. He knew many marines were quartered in nearby houses, including Major Pitcairn, one of the best-liked British officers—even by the Patriots.

Mr. Revere greeted him with the smile he always wore. "Young Lankford. You must be here about the delivery. I heard only an hour ago that it arrived safely."

"Delivery?" Stephen stared at him blankly. "Oh, the delivery!" He must be speaking about his father and Will. They were safe! Joy and relief flooded him in spite of the hard news he carried.

"Thank you, sir, but that isn't why I'm here." Stephen whispered Lieutenant Andrews's message.

Mr. Revere nodded. "I've heard the same from two other sources."

Stephen felt let down. "You already knew."

"To hear it from more than one Observer only makes it more likely the news is true. It was brave of you to come. Tell no one else," Mr. Revere warned.

Would Mr. Revere ride again tonight for the Sons of Liberty? Stephen wondered. If he did, he'd have to sneak past the soldiers at the Neck or the warships in the harbor.

If there was war, would Will and the other minutemen face the officers who had been living in their homes? Lieutenant Andrews had shared his army's secret, but he hadn't said he would desert and become a Patriot. Could Andrews shoot at Will, or Will at him?

Stephen's stomach tightened. *If I have to fight, could I shoot at him? Would he shoot at me?* It was strange to not only share his home with the enemy, but to like him as well.

When Stephen turned the corner near his house, he saw Dr. Cuyler's carriage leaving. To his surprise, Dan was on a horse beside the carriage. "Dr. Cuyler!" He sprinted down the street. "Were you looking for me, Doctor?"

Dr. Cuyler quickly told him that Dan's father was ill. Dr. Cuyler thought he might need to operate on Dan's father at his farm. "If that's true, I'll need your help, Stephen."

Stephen glanced at Dan's face. His usual easygoing smile was gone. Worry sat in the eyes that met his.

Stephen hurried into the house to tell his mother where he'd be and to grab a jacket, for the nice spring day would turn into a cool evening.

Mother followed him out to the carriage. "Are you sure you need Stephen with you tonight, Cuyler?"

"I need him, Maggie."

"There are so many soldiers about tonight. I hate to have Stephen out."

"I'll watch out for him, Maggie. I promise."

Her hand clutched the side of the carriage. For a minute Stephen thought she wouldn't let him leave with her younger brother.

Finally she nodded and stepped back. "I hope your father will be all right, Dan."

"Thank you, ma'am."

The wheels clattered over the cobblestones. Stephen looked back. His mother was still standing in front of the house, staring after them.

"It would save us a lot of time if we could take the Charlestown ferry from the north end of Boston," Dr. Cuyler grumbled. "Instead we have to go south across the Neck, then north. It will take us twice as long to get there. I hope the extra time won't cost Dan's father his life."

There was a moment at the Neck when Stephen didn't think they'd be allowed to leave Boston. The guards had told Dr. Cuyler that he could leave, but not Stephen or Dan. Dr. Cuyler convinced them that Dan's father was truly ill, that Dan was needed to show him the way to the farm, and that he needed Stephen to assist him.

A lantern swung from each side of the carriage roof, helping light the way for the horses. The night sounds of owls, insects, and toads kept them company.

They'd been driving a long time when Stephen looked across the river toward Boston. He could see campfires on the common and candlelit windows.

He pointed out two lights, higher than any others, to Dr. Cuyler and Dan. "Someone must have hung lanterns in the tower of Christ Church," he said. "Isn't that strange?"

Chapter 16

War!

When they arrived at the farmhouse, Dr. Cuyler grabbed his black bag. "Stephen, help Dan with the horses. See you're quick about it. Bring the medicine chest."

Stephen had been worrying about something all the way from Boston. Mr. Revere had told him not to tell anyone else Lieutenant Andrews's secret, but the silversmith hadn't known Stephen would be leaving town that night, traveling the very road the British would likely travel to reach Concord. He hadn't known Stephen would be at a farmhouse just outside Lexington, the town the redcoats would have to pass through on their way.

Dan was helping Stephen unhitch Dr. Cuyler's horses from the carriage. Stephen took a deep breath. "Dan, can you get a message to the minutemen around here?"

Dan's hands froze on the reins. "Tonight?"

Stephen nodded, darting a look over his shoulder at the farmhouse. Dr. Cuyler had already gone inside. Stephen told Dan Lieutenant Andrews's secret while they took the horses to the barn to be fed, watered, and brushed down.

"Guess I'm not too surprised," Dan said. "This afternoon the minutemen were called to Lexington Green when British officers were spotted on the roads. When none of our lookouts saw troops coming, the men were sent home."

He grinned at Stephen across the horse's back. "If the redcoats are figurin' to find any guns at Concord, they're goin' to be mightily disappointed."

"Why?"

"Paul Revere warned the Concord Patriots on Sunday that the redcoats were beginnin' to act a might suspicious, pullin' men off duty to train. Concord seemed the likely place for the redcoats to head. The Massachusetts Congress was meetin' there. Would've been easy for Gage's men to arrest all the most powerful Patriot leaders in Massachusetts. Then, too, it's the nearest place to Boston with a good supply of ammunition and guns."

"How do you find out so much, Dan?"

"Livin' in the country isn't like livin' in Boston. We don't have redcoats tellin' us what we can and can't do and livin' in our houses. We don't have to worry 'bout the redcoats overhearin' us if we talk 'bout Patriot doin's. Sunday I visited cousins in Concord. We had a grand time hidin' things."

"Hiding what things?"

"Ammunition and guns, of course." He snorted. "The redcoats will never find them. We dropped bags of bullets in the swamps, and we buried the cannons in a farmer's field."

Stephen burst out laughing at the thought of a farmer plowing over cannons.

When the horses were cared for, Dan saddled his father's only other horse. Then he raced toward the house to check on his father. Soon he was back carrying an old squirrel gun.

"We'll stop those redcoats," he told Stephen. He swung himself up onto his horse's back. His horse whinnied in protest as Dan wheeled him about to head down the lane. "Thanks for the warnin', friend."

He was off. Would he warn the minutemen in time to truly stop the redcoats? Stephen wondered.

Dr. Cuyler frowned at him when he finally went inside. "I thought I told you to hurry." He didn't waste time with more scolding. Instead he quickly told Stephen what was wrong with Dan's father. He was going to operate, and Stephen would need to help.

He took instruments from his black bag and laid them on the kitchen table, where he'd be operating. Stephen hurried out of his cloak and into the black apron that protected his vest and breeches from blood.

The fireplace's heat warmed away the chill from his night ride. Like all kitchen fireplaces, it was as wide as he was tall, and almost as high. He could smell cornmeal mush cooking slowly in the large black kettle hanging from a crane over the low flames. It reminded him that he hadn't eaten since noon. There was no time to think of food now. He must work.

About two in the morning, when a horse's hooves were heard slamming against the dirt farm lane, Stephen and Dr. Cuyler didn't even look up from their patient. A moment later a man called, "The redcoats are coming! Patriots turn out!" Then the sound of hooves headed back down the lane.

Dr. Cuyler glanced across the wooden table at Stephen in the light of the lanterns that hung from the kitchen rafters. Stephen looked back at him without saying a word. Then they both went back to work. The redcoats and minutemen might be planning to meet, but their duty now was to save the man in front of them.

Blam! Blam! Blam!

Stephen's head jerked up. "Gunfire!" Dr. Cuyler exclaimed. "The locals must be waking the countryside, letting them know the redcoats are coming."

Soon they heard a bell ringing. Dan's mother said it was the bell from a church at Lexington. Another way to wake the people. Before long other church bells from nearby villages joined in. The gong of bells kept up all night.

It was about four in the morning when Dr. Cuyler drew the last stitch, closing the operation. Dan's father was still alive. Now if only he didn't develop a serious infection.

Dan's mother gave them cornmeal mush for breakfast. To pay for the operation, she gave Dr. Cuyler a large smoked ham. Stephen put it in the trunk the doctor kept on the back of his carriage. Dan's mother wrapped in rags two stones she'd heated in the fireplace. Stephen and Dr. Cuyler placed them at their feet in the carriage to ward off the cold morning air.

They were on the road before four-thirty. Dogs barked and howled. Church bells still sounded through the darkness. Candles lit farmhouse windows. Dr. Cuyler and Stephen weren't the only ones on the road. Men on foot and horseback were hurrying toward Lexington.

"Fools," Dr. Cuyler muttered, slapping the reins against

the horses' flanks. "Don't they know better than to anger the king's troops?"

Stephen didn't answer. He gripped the edge of the carriage seat, swaying as the horses moved along the rutted road only a little faster than a walk. They had sixteen miles back to Boston. Stephen knew Dr. Cuyler didn't want to tire the horses too soon.

When they neared Lexington Green, where Stephen and Dan had watched the minutemen practice months before, the gray sky of dawn revealed the shadows of men in front of the meetinghouse.

The road ran alongside the green. Beyond the meetinghouse Stephen saw a dark column moving closer, growing larger and larger. "Redcoats!" he whispered hoarsely.

Dr. Cuyler urged his horses to the side of the road, beneath a large tree beside a rock wall. They would have to wait until the redcoats passed to continue.

A drum began its rat-a-tat-tat. They heard the captain order the minutemen to fall in. The men formed two lines in front of the meeting house. There were only about seventy, Stephen guessed—farmers and craftsmen from the way they were dressed. About forty townspeople looked on from doorways and windows and behind stone walls.

Was Dan with the minutemen? Stephen wondered, leaning forward on the seat to see better in the dim light. The lanterns still swung from the carriage top, but they were no help any longer. He lifted the glass sides and blew out the candles.

Two men hurried behind the minutemen, carrying a trunk. Stephen recognized one of them: Paul Revere. So he'd made it out of Boston to warn the countryside after all. Maybe Dan's warning hadn't been needed.

"Let the redcoats pass. Don't fire unless you're fired upon!" the captain called to his men.

A moment later, the redcoats marched past the meeting house and onto the green. "There are a lot more redcoats than minutemen!" Stephen said.

Dr. Cuyler nodded grimly. "Even the most hotheaded rebel wouldn't be foolish enough to fight against such odds."

Stephen saw Major Pitcairn, who was quartered with Paul Revere's neighbors. He was one of the redcoats' leaders. The redcoats stopped about 150 feet from the Patriots. Major Pitcairn rode up to the minutemen, his sword drawn. "Ye rebels, disperse! Lay down your arms! Why don't ye lay down your arms?"

There was a flash of gunpowder, the roar of a musket. Then another and another!

Stephen leaped to his feet, setting the carriage rocking. He couldn't tell who had fired first. Now both sides were firing! Gunpowder smoke filled the air.

Some minutemen scurried away, dodging redcoats' musket balls and bayonets. Some hid behind trees and walls or headed toward nearby buildings. Others stayed where they were.

The redcoats hurried after the minutemen. Bodies were falling from the musket fire! A minuteman not much older than Stephen was hit in the chest with a musket ball. He crawled away, bleeding heavily.

Major Pitcairn whirled his horse around. His sword flashed as he brought it down in a motion Stephen knew meant to stop firing. But the redcoats didn't stop firing!

Minutemen shot from the green, from behind a stone wall, and from nearby buildings.

Horrified, Stephen watched a redcoat jam the bayonet on the end of his musket into a fallen Patriot.

Major Pitcairn fell with his horse. Had the friendly officer been hit? Stephen breathed a sigh of relief when the major stood. His horse had been hit.

A musket ball whizzed by Stephen's head. Dr. Cuyler yanked him down by his coat sleeve. "Get behind the stone wall!" he ordered. Stephen tried to watch the fighting while he moved. Dr. Cuyler followed, keeping hold of the horses' reins, which wasn't easy. The bays tried to bolt, frightened by the muskets.

Minutemen raced to get away from the redcoats. Some fled down a road. Most crossed a swamp to reach safe land.

It was only minutes before the fighting was over. Stephen's anger boiled over as the redcoats cheered. How could they cheer killing and hurting people? Their officers struggled to get the troops in order again. Only one or two Redcoats had been wounded and none killed. Soon the cheerful troops set off down the road toward Concord.

Dr. Cuyler grabbed his black leather bag. "We'd best see if we can help any of these foolish rebels."

Stephen followed him. Already some of the wounded were being carried to nearby homes and Buckman's Tavern. The man Stephen had seen bayoneted was dead. So was the young man he'd seen crawling away. He'd died within feet of his own front door.

There were eight dead. Stephen was glad to see Dan wasn't among them. Nor was Dan one of the ten wounded.

The sight of the wounds almost made Stephen sick. He'd often helped Dr. Cuyler treat patients with illnesses and broken bones. He'd never treated a musket wound. He hadn't treated anyone who'd been purposely shot by someone else.

It's the wounded who are important, not me, he told himself again and again. He made himself watch carefully as Dr. Cuyler used a steel probe to find musket balls and then used a bullet extractor—shaped much like scissors—to remove them. Some day Stephen might have to do this himself. After the musket balls were removed, Dr. Cuyler let him put plasters from the medicine box on the wounds and bind them up.

They were there for hours, first helping the wounded and then eating lunch at Buckman's Tavern. While at lunch, Stephen and Dr. Cuyler were surprised when Stephen's father and William joined them, guns in their hands. Stephen found out for the first time that they'd been staying at a farm near Lexington since leaving Boston. Dr. Cuyler and Stephen were even more surprised to find the Lankfords had fought on Lexington Green!

Will looked pale. "The man next to me was killed by the redcoats. He never fired a shot. One minute he was alive and the next he was dead. You were right, Stephen, when you said it's easier to kill a man than to keep him alive."

Suddenly a man rushed in. "Redcoats are headed back this way! Concord's men are chasin' them! Patriots turn out!"

Will and Father grabbed their guns and jumped up. "We have to go," Father said. "Tell your mother we're safe, Stephen. We'll be in touch."

Stephen's heart sank as they ran into the tavern hallway and out the front door. If they kept fighting, would he ever see them alive again?

He and Dr. Cuyler left right away. They could hear gunfire coming from the road toward Concord. Dr. Cuyler wanted to get back to Boston before they were caught in the fighting.

Half a mile down the road, they ran into a fresh troop of redcoats coming from Boston. Stephen recognized young Lieutenant Percy, who was leading them. The officer often breakfasted with Mr. Hancock, the wealthy Patriot leader, after his men practiced on the common. He was a slender man with a narrow face and long, straight nose. Sunlight glinted off his red jacket's brass buttons and gold braid as he rode in front of the troops.

Lieutenant Percy stopped Dr. Cuyler and Stephen, questioning them about rumors he'd heard of fighting at Lexington. While they talked, the sound of musketfire grew louder. Then redcoats appeared, struggling down the road with minutemen on their tail.

Lieutenant Percy issued sharp orders. His men formed a square. The tired redcoats arriving from Lexington and Concord dropped to the ground inside the square to rest and let Lieutenant Percy's fresh troops take over the fighting.

Stephen had never seen such tired men as those lying on the ground. They panted. Their chests heaved. Most of them were simply worn out from running from the Patriot troops. Some were wounded. Stephen and Dr. Cuyler busied themselves caring for the wounded.

"Hello, Stephen."

He looked up in surprise. The wounded man they'd knelt beside was Lieutenant Andrews! A musket ball had hit him in the thigh.

Lieutenant Andrews was still gasping for breath. He told them a bit of what happened at Concord. The town militia had treated them politely, escorting them into town with drums and fifes. But when Major Pitcairn ordered his men to destroy a bridge, fighting started.

When the redcoats headed back to Lexington along the tree-lined road, the minutemen and other colonials had kept up a constant fire. The redcoats had been sitting ducks in the middle of the road while the minutemen shot from behind trees, bushes, fences, and sometimes from houses.

"We didn't stand a chance," Lieutenant Andrews said, gritting his teeth against the pain as Dr. Cuyler removed the musket ball. "Many of our soldiers have been killed or wounded."

So the redcoats had "won" the battle on Lexington Green, Stephen thought, but the Patriots were "winning" the rest of the battle.

The Patriot who had shot Lieutenant Andrews would never know that the officer had tried to help the Patriots by telling Stephen the redcoats' plans, Stephen thought as he and Dr. Cuyler moved on to another wounded man. Musket fire and orders yelled by officers continued while they worked.

Lieutenant Percy's men had two cannons. They fired them toward the minutemen, who scattered. Their old squirrel and duck guns were no match for such bigger weapons.

Lieutenant Percy sent some of his men to nearby farms for carts and horses for the wounded soldiers. In less than an hour, the redcoats were moving again, headed back toward Charlestown, where their boats were tied. Dr. Cuyler and Stephen were ordered to join them. The wounded redcoats needed them.

"There will be no turning back now," Dr. Cuyler said grimly as they rode in the carriage in the midst of the troops.

Questions ran through Stephen's mind. What would happen next? How many minutemen and redcoats would die or be maimed? What would happen between friends and families who were on opposite sides of the conflict? How would the redcoats treat Patriots in Boston? Would the Patriots be safe?

The time Stephen had dreaded for so long had come. He gripped the edge of the seat until his fingers hurt. "It's a war now. I'll have to fight."

Dr. Cuyler sighed. "Very likely. At fifteen, you're a man now."

"I'm not sure I'm ready."

"To be a man, or to fight? You've no choice in one and little in the other."

Stephen lifted his chin. "I learned one thing today. Battlefields are a place of killing, but a place of saving lives, too. If I have to fight, I'll have to carry a gun, but I want to carry a doctor's tools, too. Maybe I can be a doctor's helper for the army. Will you teach me all you can?"

It was strange, Stephen thought, asking his Loyalist uncle to teach him to save the lives of his enemies, the minutemen.

"You don't know nearly enough yet," Dr. Cuyler said. "There isn't time to teach you everything. But yes, I'll teach you what I can in the short time we have. May God help you. May He help us all."

What would Anna think when she heard the war had started, Stephen wondered? Would she wonder whether she could have stopped it by telling General Gage about Lieutenant Andrews and Stephen?

Today Dr. Cuyler had helped wounded minutemen on Lexington Green. Stephen had worked beside his uncle helping wounded redcoats. He and Dr. Cuyler liked each other. He was sure they always would. Just like his parents and Dr. Cuyler would always like each other, even though none of their lives would ever be the same again.

The sound of muskets started again. Minutemen were

shooting at the redcoats. The redcoats began firing back. Stephen felt years older than when he'd left Boston the night before.

One thing for sure, Stephen thought, *after seeing the wounded and dead on both sides, I know I can't stand by and watch while others fight for my rights. I have to fight for my own rights. Maybe God gave me the wish to be a doctor so I can help save the lives of other Patriots in this war.*

His fingers closed over the silver whistle in his pocket. Stephen sat up a little straighter. One way or another, a person always had to fight for what he believed.

There's More!

The American Adventure continues with *The American Victory*. Paul Lankford's father is a stranger. Off fighting the Revolutionary War, Paul's father has rarely been home during the past six years. Now that's changing. The fighting is over, America has won, and Paul's father is home.

Paul knows he should love his father, but how can he love a person he doesn't even know? He's much more comfortable discussing ships with his Uncle Ethan or playing with his cousin Maggie than he is listening to his own father go on about politics.

Paul's tried everything he can think of to make the relationship right, but nothing seems to work. What will it take for Paul to be able to love his father?